Also by Benilde Little

*Acting Out*
*The Itch*
*Good Hair*

# Who Does She Think She Is?

*A Novel*

## BENILDE LITTLE

FREE PRESS
New York   London   Toronto   Sydney

FREE PRESS
A Division of Simon & Schuster, Inc.
1230 Avenue of the Americas
New York, NY 10020

FREE PRESS and colophon are trademarks of Simon & Schuster, Inc.

For information about special discounts for bulk purchases, please contact Simon & Schuster Special Sales: 1-800-456-6798 or business@simonandschuster.com

DESIGNED BY LAUREN SIMONETTI

Manufactured in the United States of America

1   3   5   7   9   10   8   6   4   2

Library of Congress Cataloging-in-Publication Data
Little, Benilde
Who does she think she is : a novel / Benilde Little
p. cm.
1. African American families—Fiction. 2. African American women—Fiction. 3. Mothers and daughters—Fiction. 4. Interracial marriage—Fiction. 5. Race relations—Fiction. 6. Social classes—Fiction. 7. Weddings—Fiction. 8. New York (N.Y.)—Fiction 9. Newport (R.I.)—Fiction.
I. Title.
PS3562.I78276 W47 2005
813'.54—dc22   2004061974

ISBN 0-684-85482-1

*For Faith,*
I couldn't have done this without you.

Elegance is refusal.

—Diana Vreeland


Your crown has been bought and paid for.

—James Baldwin

# Acknowledgments

Thanks to my parents, Clara and Matthew Little; my girlfriends Joni Brown, Wendy Rountree, Eleanore Wells, Lynne Toye, Monique Greenwood; my writer/sisters Christina Baker Kline, Alice Elliott Dark, Pamela Redmond Satran; artist/sister Iqua Colson. Thank you to my unwaveringly supportive editor, Dominick Anfuso. Thanks to Deborah Medeiros Baker for pulling together the shoot. Thanks to Ted and Nina Wells for the wonderful *Acting Out* party; Dr. Bob and Joan Austin for hosting the great signing in Houston and E. Lynn Harris for the Atlanta party that got snowed out. My friend and agent Faith Hampton Childs, who just understands; my babies, precious Baldwin and Ford, for keeping my heart open; and my husband and biggest supporter, Cliff Virgin, the perfect blend of Miles and Jack, who adds fullness and fun to my life and constantly pushes me to write it down!

# Who
# Does She
# Think
# She Is?

*Aisha Branch McCovney, daughter of Camille Branch and stepdaughter of Lemuel McCovney of Llewellyn Park, will marry Harrison "Will" Fitzhugh, son of Meredith Powell Fitzhugh Martin of New York and Venice and William Garrison Fitzhugh of New York and Millbrook. The couple will wed at the groom's family home in Newport, Rhode Island next June.*

*The bride, twenty-six, graduated from Newark Academy in Livingston and cum laude from the University of Virginia, and is an assistant media buyer with Rowe/Day, the advertising firm. The groom, twenty-seven, graduated from Harvard and the Sorbonne, and is an art director at the same firm, which is where the couple met.*

*The bride's stepfather is the senior partner of the law firm McCovney, Lewis & Brown, in East Orange. The bride's mother is the head of social work at the Newark Emergency Services for Children.*

*The bridegroom's father is a private investor. The bridegroom's mother is a painter. The bridegroom's great-grandfather, Garrison Granger Fitzhugh, was founding partner of the Continental Insurance Company; his grandfather, Granger William Fitzhugh, was CEO. The groom's maternal great-grandfather founded Mercantile Steel.*

Geneva sighed and neatly folded a copy of the hometown newspaper, placing it on the kitchen table so that Mabel, the lady who comes twice a week to tidy things up a bit, could see the announcement. *Baby girl getting married,* Mabel would say. *Seems like just yesterday she was runnin' through this house wit' me yellin' after her to slow down. Always was in a rush. That little girl was someum' else. Marrying a White boy, a rich White boy. You go 'head, Miss I-esh-a. Miss Geneva can die a happy woman now—her grandbaby finally doing it right,* she'd say, always emphasizing the *I* sound at the beginning of her name, *I-e-sha,* driving Geneva crazy in the process.

The phones started ringing, as Geneva knew they would once the news landed in the *Beacon-Herald.*

"Yes, Pearl, that's my little Aisha. Mm-hmm, she's twenty-six already. I know, seems like we just had her christened."

"Yes, I'm very pleased. He's a very nice young man, comes from a very respectable family."

"Well, I know, you seeing more and more of it these days. The girls say there just aren't that many of our men to go around, you know, who are going on, finishing their education and stretching themselves."

"Yes, I suppose you're right. It's a different world."

"Alright now, mmmm, and thank you for calling. Yes, see you at church."

"'Bye now."

She hung up her kitchen wall phone.

There was still a lot to be done. Camille is so lackadaisical. You have to stay on her about every detail. She was supposed to start calling florists to get estimates. She gets so caught up with her so-called clients and tryin' to save the world, she'd forget her own head if it wasn't attached and if it didn't have all that hair and mess everywhere.

Geneva exhaled in exasperation, as she'd been doing for most of Camille's forty-five years. She took a last sip of tea and put the cup in the sink, turned on the water and swirled it around the ring in the cup.

At seventy she had more energy than many twenty years younger.

"Ew, look at the time," she said to no one. "I'm going to be late for service."

Geneva would not be late; she never was, for anything. What she would be was not early. She'd already laid out what she was going to wear—her coral suit, matching hat, beige pumps, hose and purse.

She was alone now in the high ranch she and her late husband, Major, had bought with an eye toward their twilight years. Now, the wide halls and spacious rooms were too much for just one person, but she couldn't bring herself to part with it. If she really tried she could still smell Major's aftershave in the master bath and the smell comforted her, just the way she liked—in private.

Geneva wheeled her late model Buick around the church parking lot, mumbling curse words because her usual parking space was taken, as were all the choice spots. And to add insult, she didn't even know the offender. Used to be time when she knew everybody who was a member of First Presbyterian, but now they got all kinds of new people coming in, driving these awful trucks, vans, SUBs, whatever they're called, taking up two spaces. It's just abominable. Camille and Lem of course had one and had the nerve to be a Cadillac—it's just foolishness. Geneva ended up having to park on the street. Walking up to the church, seeing it from the front, she was struck by how beautiful the architecture was and for a moment she felt sad that Aisha wouldn't be getting married there. It would be nice to continue the tradition, but what was she talking about, Camille killed that idea a long time ago, going and getting herself in trouble like some common . . .

The sedate organ music took Geneva's mind off her daughter for a while and she smiled as she walked down the aisle to her seat in the third pew, right aisle. She mouthed thank-yous to the ladies who wordlessly complimented her hat, and sat down.

Marjorie Blessitt sang "How Blessed Thou Art" and Geneva let the music soothe her soul.

# CHAPTER 1

## Aisha

Aisha rolled over in her bed to pick up her cell phone—Will had programmed it to play "Here Comes the Bride." She'd been out with her best friend Cedra, drinking mojitos till three in the morning, and was in no mood to wake up now.

"Hello. This better be good," she whispered hoarsely.

"Girl, they all talking about you at home, you all up in the *Beacon-Observer* today," Cedra said.

"What're you talking about? Why are you up?"

"You know I never sleep late, plus Mom called me up all excited about your engagement announcement."

"Oh, oh shit, I'd forgotten all about that. Do you have it?"

"No, Mom saw it and said that's all everybody was talking about at early service this morning. Apparently they didn't know Will was White."

"You're kidding."

"Nope, that's what Mom said."

"Well, what did the picture look like?"

Aisha knew what the words would say—she wrote them—

but she wanted to see what the picture looked like. Will didn't want to do a posed picture so they sent in several from a weekend at Will's grandmother's place in the Hamptons, Georgica Pond. She was worried about looking too greasy; what her hair was going to look like; were they going to look like yet another dorky we-are-the-world, we-met-at-Bard couple.

"Mom said it was a nice picture. You can look at it online."

"Good idea, I'll call you back."

Aisha went to her computer, which sat on her dining room table, which doubled as her desk and sat in the middle of her Manhattan studio apartment. Good placement, she noted, slightly above the fold, very good. Will looks cute, he photographs very well, his dark hair is not too short and his mother's dreamy eyes jump off the page. Yeah. Her hair hadn't frizzed out too much and she and Will did not look like a Benetton ad. His tan and her lack of one put them only a shade or two apart. It looked casual, but not too. Will hates anything studied. "I don't know what he's going to do when we move in together and he sees how long it takes me to achieve my unstudied look."

She smiled as she read the announcement. Yes, he's cute, he's successful and he comes from money and it ain't new. Yesss, she hissed to herself, doing an "I'm bad" bop into the kitchenette to make a cup of chai tea. Ignoring the slight pounding around her temples, she tied the belt of her stretch terry robe around her waist and sat back at the computer, scanning her e-mails. Nothing urgent.

She opened *The New York Times,* sat in her favorite chenille armchair and scanned the wedding announcements. In June and September there was big-time competition for space. She'd already begun to compose the actual wedding announcement, thinking about how she and Will had met, trying to come up with something different enough to wield them the big story in the vows section.

Of all people to introduce us, she thought, Belinda Carlyle had to be the tightest White woman under thirty in America. She'd gone to UVA with Belinda and they ended up at the same agency.

*Anyway, being nice, I agreed to have lunch with her one day so we're walking out of the building and Will is barreling in and almost bumps into me. Will's all distracted, says sorry and keeps going and Belinda calls after him.*

*"Fitzhugh, is that you?"*

*Will turns around, big old grin 'cause he knows anybody who calls him by his last name is someone from way back.*

*"Belinda Carlyle, what's up?"*

*He hugs her and she turns a shade pinker.*

*She's grinning so hard she seems drunk. They do the "how you been, who've you seen?" before they or he realizes that I'm standing there and they're being rude.*

*Will looks at me, his perfectly orthodontically rendered teeth gleaming.*

*He sticks his hand out and says, "Hi, I'm Will."*

*"Oh, forgive me," Belinda breathes all fake, but needing me to believe that she'd just forgotten her manners.*

*"Will Fitzhugh, meet Aisha McCovney, Aisha Branch McCovney."*

*Will and I shake hands.*

*"Will and I went to Andover together. Aisha and I were at UVA together. We were just going to lunch, do you . . . ?"*

*"Nah, nah. I can't, but maybe another time. You're here?"*

*"Yes, I'm in accounts."*

*"I'm a media buyer," I insert.*

*I still don't know why I was so forward with him. I'd never really been into White boys before, but this one, he was clearly someone to make an exception for.*

"Cool. Well, it was great to see you, Belinda. Another time, we can . . ." He nodded at me, "Nice to meet you Aisha."

"You too, Will."

"I'll call you about lunch," Belinda calls after him.

Belinda and I go to an overpriced joint across the street from our building and I'm convinced she's oozing. We sit down and I'm trying hard not to jump her with questions about Will.

"So, I didn't know you went to boarding school," I start.

Belinda studies the menu, searching for something specific.

"Yes, only for my last three years. I had been at a parochial school." She closed her menu.

Why am I not surprised?

"Do you know what you want?" she asked.

I wanted to say, Will's phone number, but resisted.

"Yes, I'm having a cheeseburger. You wanna split some fries?"

She looks at me like I said, Can I split your thighs?

"I can't eat like that. I'd be huge. You're such a stick."

Oh, another average-weight girl who obsesses about her food intake. It's so boring.

"So, how's the account side?" I say, changing the subject.

"It's okay, not really what I want to be doing, but . . . I'll have a Diet Coke and the Cobb salad, no bacon, no eggs and dressing on the side."

The waitress took our orders and left.

"Um, so what was I . . . Oh yeah, I think I might go back to school. I really want to teach."

"Really? Like what, high school, college?"

I was bored out of my mind.

"No, elementary, maybe like second or third, early where I could really make a difference."

"Wow, Belinda, that's great. You should do it . . ." I say, feeling sorry for herds of her future eight-year-old pupils.

"So, you and what was that guy's name . . . ?"

"Will?"

"Yes, Will. You went to school together?"

"Um, yeah."

*She's going to make me work.*

"And he works at Rowe?"

"Apparently."

"He's in?"

"Art . . . copy."

*Bingo. I just needed a department.*

# CHAPTER 2

## My Weddin' Had to Be Discreet

## *Camille*

I sat at my desk staring over a pile of files that were stacked on a corner of my always messy space. I looked out the window, although there wasn't much to look at on a Sunday in downtown Newark. I zoned out, watching the garage attendant watch a mini-television. Mostly I was thinking about the engagement announcement; my child, my baby, was getting married. The announcement sat folded on my desk as my thoughts meandered and I looked down at the photograph of my gorgeous Aisha smiling, brimming with confidence, and noted how little she had changed. She always knew exactly what she wanted, even as a baby, and wouldn't veer. If she wanted the pink one but the pink ones weren't available and I offered the blue, she'd say never mind, I don't want blue, and that would be that. No tantrum, no second thoughts, just very clear about what she wanted and how. How can she be twenty-six? Where in the hell does the time go? It's not like I feel as if I haven't lived these forty-five years, but the ones spent mothering, which has been my entire adult life, have zoomed by. I certainly have the gray hairs—everywhere—and the flab to prove it even though my friends who don't have kids don't. They've stood time still and not having a breathing, growing human living with you, reminding you that the years are clicking by, it's possible, I suppose. They also have time to go to the gym. Even my friends who had kids later and with a partner look younger and Mother Geneva never lets it pass that she saw so-and-so from Jack and Jill who looked so good and young and then she looks at me and I can just hear the *tsk-tsk*ing. Oh, how you let yourself go. I hate that she doesn't seem to understand that there was no time for me. I was working, taking care of Aisha, trying to give her everything and more, the best education, clothes, cultural outings, trying to take care of what she was going to need, not me. I was on autopilot raising her by myself for the first five years, till I met Lem, and even then I still felt like I had something to prove by having had the nerve to be a single mother. I'd just been too busy to notice me.

After I locked my hair and stopped having my twice-a-month sessions with Millie, who'd go on about my roots having their own zip code and let me wax those brows before we change your name to Frieda and where are you going wearing that muumuu, there was no one to even point out how I looked. I wear loose-fitting, unconstructed clothes and you really can forget about having a waistline when you dress like I do. Lem didn't seem to care one way or the other as long as he was getting regular sex and meals. I used to be thin, never as skinny as my child, and now I'm squeezing into 16s. It's a body I don't even recognize. I've started walking every day and hopefully that'll help. Aisha says there are no good mother-of-the-bride dresses in my size and lately has been sending me brochures for Weight Watchers. Her point has been well taken—she don't want no overweight mama at her wedding, and I frankly don't want to be, but there's the other part of me that says, I'm forty-five and I really just don't give a damn.

Aisha is as a woman as she was as a baby—highly demanding but generally very sweet. This wedding is going to be fabulous, even if it kills a few of us in the process. Lem, who has never said no to her, is even getting fed up with her, asking for a wedding gown that costs seven thousand dollars—it's criminal, it's almost what my clients live on in a year. I just can't see it. Aisha really has no sense of how much that is. She's seen the numbers Lem has won in client settlements, not realizing that he only gets a third and has to split that with his partners and pay upkeep on the firm. Her education, private school almost since kindergarten and then college, cost us . . . well, I don't even want to think about it. The planets aligned for her when she met Will, 'cause God knows she needed to marry rich. I often wonder how the hell I ended up with a daughter like this—where she got all her materialism and grandiosity. She saw me dragging myself through school, working at night at the post office to pay for it all—for camp and lessons and exchange trips to Spain and France. Allowing her grandparents to pick up the tab only when I simply could not and she just had to have that ski trip, outfit, year abroad. Well, that's where she got a lot of it. I'm the only one in this child's life who can and does say no to her and of course I'm big bad Mommy. She's been blessed with knockout looks—thank God she wasn't tall because she would've been a model; my definition of death by shallowness. People were constantly telling me that she should be a model, stopping us on the streets of Manhattan when she was an adolescent, handing me cards for this agency or that magazine. There was no way I was going to turn my child into some kind of brown Brooke Shields—we had enough theater in our lives. I didn't need to add stage mother to my résumé. The problem with being beautiful and educated is that you don't have to ever really work for anything. Geneva feels that Aisha shouldn't have to, that that's why we did, but I don't agree with her. It's obviously one of the many things we disagree about. I think everyone should have to work, to strive for some kind of achievement beyond things that land in your lap, like good looks and well-to-do parents. Geneva feels that way too but none of this applies to her perfect Aisha.

I never dreamed of the big fairy-tale wedding, even before it was clear that I wouldn't be having one. Geneva was very clear that when I did get married it had to be "discreet"—after all, I was already a mother and it was just unseemly to do otherwise. I thought she was going to have a coronary when she saw Mayor Giuliani with his new bride (not her first altar trip), in a whitish wedding dress and a tiara. "That woman should be shot at dawn for carrying on like that . . . they're just heathens," she'd said. I always felt a little guilty for cheating Lem out of his chance to have the big splashy wedding. He would've loved it, all that glad-handing and partying. He said he didn't miss it, but I know that's part of the reason he's writing the big checks for Aisha's wedding. Even though he's her stepfather and we're divorced now, he's raised her as his own. I guess the planets lined up for me too.

Our wedding was held at the home of a judge who Lem had clerked for when he was right out of law school. Judge Pierce is a father figure to Lem. Our wedding was charming. It was in the Pierces' garden, the peonies were in full bloom; we had cocktails and hors d'oeuvres on the patio. I wore an apricot brocade suit and Lem wore a blue pinstripe; Aisha was my maid of honor and flower girl. She took her role very seriously and Lem kissed both of us after the you-may-now-kiss-the-bride part.

I met Lem when I was getting my master's. He was teaching an undergraduate criminal-law class and one night he came out of the school and saw me flooding the battery of my ten-year-old Datsun B210, trying to get it to start. The first thing that struck me about him was how kind he was, and country. He had a big wide-open childlike smile and stopped just short of calling me ma'am—which shortly began to drive me insane. He gave my car a jump and then invited me to go for a drink at the Gateway Hilton Hotel. I could go only because Aisha was with my parents on the nights I had classes. Geneva insisted on it and she'd take her to school the next day. So, off I went like the free unencumbered girl I never was and sat with Lem talking until they closed the place. We went from cocktails to coffee in that sitting and while he wasn't fine he was strong and had a clarity that I needed. I knew that he was going to be in my life in some way. He was thirty-three. I was twenty-six. He'd never been married—too busy building his practice. He was the only boy in a family of four sisters, born in Georgia but raised in Newark, where his parents had migrated. He went to college and law school on an academic scholarship. We married two years to the day after we met and ours was the kind of marriage I knew it would be—steady. Lem worked all the time and provided us with material comforts many women would drool over. We lived in a French-style colonial with seven bedrooms and a carriage house in a gated community. In the early years we'd rent out the carriage house to law students, and later opened it to various family members on Lem's side, whenever any of them needed a place to stay. When we married we both assumed we would have children together but it never happened and the doctors couldn't figure out why, other than Lem's parts were in working order. Again I felt bad for Lem and even offered to divorce him so that he could marry someone who could give him children. He said I offended him, that Aisha and I were all that he needed. You are my family. Seven years later, we amicably decided to end our commitment.

Aisha called to tell me that *Town and Country* was planning to "cover" the event. This is so far from where I was at her age—other than the fact that I was already a mother, in my day weddings weren't this big traditional thing, we were just coming out of rejecting everything establishment—weddings and marriage at the top of the list. But Princess Diana and Vera Wang, founder of wedding-dress chic, ushered in a return to all this wedding hoopla twenty years ago and it shows no sign of reversing. When my Spelman roommates married in the early 1980s they had the whole hog too, big rings, the long trains, all the stuff Aisha assumes she should have.

As for my life, my career, I've been alone for a long time, before, during and after Lem. Being a teenage mother cut me off from my peers who were pledging when I was finger painting, setting up first apartments while I was going to PTA meetings. I'd had a famous musician father, a sometime haughty mother who left my brother and me to basically fend for ourselves way before we were prepared and tried to disown both of us when we failed to live up to her desired life of Negro respectability. My brother MJ, short for Major Junior, first *quit his good job as a Wall Street lawyer and moved halfway across the country to work, as what, Ernest and Julio Gallo and he's what, oh no, no son of mine* . . . to add insult to injury is whaaat—gay? Poor, poor Geneva, who has done so much for her children to have them both turn out to be such disappointments—a fag and a teenage mother. Since Lem and I split up and Aisha moved out, I just have my work at the center to fill up my days. I enjoy my work, if you can use that word when you're talking about children being found abandoned in basements, eighteen-year-old mothers of three and four kids, all different fathers and on and on; but every now and then when I can help one girl-mother get a G.E.D. and go on to college, to stop at one baby and begin a life that she owns, then there's nothing like that feeling. Geneva says I'm a classic bleeding heart *just like your daddy, always wasting time helping folks that should be helping themselves.*

In addition to being on me about my weight, Aisha's been hinting around for me to cut my hair. I've been wearing locks now for a while—has it been ten years? She says my look *is played,* that I need to get "unstuck," in the eighties. Having the hair hang down my back makes me feel womanly and since I've never been into putting chemicals in my hair to straighten it, it works for me. I wanted to kill Geneva when she combed a perm through Aisha's hair when she was ten without even asking me—knowing I didn't want that. She's been wearing it bone straight ever since. Thank God she finally stopped flicking it. When she was in elementary school, she'd be flinging and fingering imaginary hair behind the ear because she saw all her little White girlfriends at school doing it and decided it was an affect for her. That was when I let Geneva talk me into putting her in Jack and Jill. She needed to be around some other brown girls with immobile hair. It turned out to be where she met her lifelong best friend Cedra—a rock of sanity in Aisha's life. Cedra's a princess too, but a grounded one with goals that don't end with china patterns or Vineyard houses. Cedra was at our house so much when Aisha was growing up that she had her own bed. Her parents went through an ugly divorce a little after Lem and me, and if Aisha was distraught over ours, Cedra was traumatized. Our house was her safe haven where she could feel free to talk about the pain she was in, something she wouldn't share with her parents. They were clearly going through their own stuff, since the father left the mother for the mother's "best friend." Yes, it was ugly. Cedra shared much of it with us, me especially. She's now an architect working for a firm in the city and getting her final certifications. Aisha worries that Cedra is too concentrated on her career and uses it as an excuse to not be involved in life. I love it when my little one plays amateur shrink, sometimes she's right on the money, but I don't know about this one. Aisha has a hard time understanding a focus on work. I do miss the long conversations I used to have with Cedra since she's finished graduate school. I worry that with marrying this Will, Aisha will never know what it's like to feel deeply satisfied by one's work.

# CHAPTER 3

# He Sorta Got Me

## *Aisha*

Will and I did a cat-and-mouse thing for almost a year before we finally started officially dating. I'd run into him in the design department, make up excuses to have to talk to him about some inane project, my excuses so bad eventually I'm sure he saw right through them and decided to ask me out to just get rid of me—at least that's probably what he told his friends. Our first date, after too many drunken nights with his preppy friends and my bappy ones at fake low-down bars on the East Side, happened on a Friday night after work. I was dressed in my favorite cream Chloe coat, Catherine Malandrino red skirt and Loulou de la Falaise necklace. My hair and makeup perfectly done to look as if I'd just played a game of tennis. I met him in the lobby of our work building and he looked at me and said *wow*. Just the response I was going for. We went to a restaurant called the Brownstone. They had one seating a night, so you went there to linger as long as you liked and we did. Although we'd been out in groups before, this was our first one-on-one and we covered a lot of ground for a first date. He told me about growing up being bounced between his mother and father, their assorted husbands and girlfriends and careers and houses. I needed a flowchart to keep them all straight: the mother's husbands that he'd liked; the ones he'd despised; the father's girlfriends who were nice; the ones who'd come on to him. Still, I thought Will's life looked like a fairy tale or a least straight out of the pages of *Vanity Fair*—sailing camp in the Caribbean, horseback riding on the grandparents' estate, schooling in Switzerland. He was amazingly normal, considering.

"I work hard at it. It's what I've always wanted to be," he said that night. I think I fell for him at that moment. For him, normal was taking a peanut butter and jelly sandwich for lunch to public school in some nice but not too ritzy suburb, having friendships from kindergarten. Some of the stuff I'd had and maybe that was what drew him to me. The opposite, I'd admit to no one, was true for me.

In the beginning he used to compliment me so much on my appearance it made me nervous—your skin is so soft, your face is perfect, your body should be sculpted—I'm sure he was talking about my butt, because other than that, my body is just like any other stick-figure White girl he'd been with. Neither of us had ever been seriously involved with a person outside our race. He'd had a fling with a Japanese girl in college and I'd gone on a few dates with a foreign exchange student from Sweden. We'd both had lots of flirtations, but I think when we met we were ready to try for something a little deeper, a little more. We had an attraction to each other, but we'd also connected over the desire to be "normal" and we found we just liked being around each other. I got Will and he sort of got me. We'd each had to struggle with appearing one way on the outside and being totally different inside. He seemed like a privileged preppy who didn't take anything seriously and I seemed like a pampered princess who only cared about my hair. We were both so used to being underestimated that we'd given up trying to dissuade people long ago. How we trusted each other enough to be ourselves is still a mystery to me. What probably happened was we each figured the other was so far from the people we were expected to be with that we just didn't bother putting on the face, so it was easy to see underneath 'cause we weren't trying to hide.

The reaction to us getting married has been interesting. Some of Will's friends have said, *Of course he'd marry a Black woman; Will's always trying to be different.* Some (Belinda Carlyle, who's so jealous she can hardly look at me) have begun referring to me as Will's first wife in that preppy brand of humor. They say these things in front of me and continuing on in their tradition we laugh along with them, when inside I want to scream. Once, some of the girls even confronted me in the ladies' room of a downtown nightclub and said the word was that I'd thrown myself at Will.

I'm in the mirror, reapplying my new Nars gloss and here they come, like they're going to jump me, not knowing I know people who really do get jumped in the ladies' room and that I know how to defend myself. "And you're point would be?" I said, looking at the trio of Hilton sister look-alikes in the mirror.

"Well, Will is like major . . ."

"And what, I'm not supposed to have a major guy?"

I turned around to face them all.

"It's just that—"

I cut the stupid bitch off.

"I have the best because I am the best and if you got a problem with that, you can share it with someone who gives a fuck."

I turned my head dramatically enough that my freshly blown-out hair did a little whip as I walked out the door.

These bitches have no idea. I've been fighting my whole life. Fighting White people saying and doing things all in the name of keeping me in a place, and Black people for the same reason. I wasn't having that from the time I was six and the ballet teacher told my mom that my butt was too high to ever properly dance ballet. I watched Camille listen and nod and proceed to tell that teacher that she had no idea what she was talking about. Mom took me out of that class and put me in another—with a master ballet teacher who it turned out knew Grandpa. I got understudy to the lead in the spring production—high booty and all—and tore it down when the lead got strep throat.

My friends, particularly the brothers from my Jack and Jill and camp days, are also in my face.

"A White boy, Isha? A White boy?" It's become something like a greeting. My girls understand—either they are on the it's-just-love-tip, or they're like, *A sister's gotta do what a sister's gotta do.* Translation: There ain't enough Black men out there.

Of course the truth of the matter is that it's all that and more. The reason people marry is complicated enough when their skin looks the same—from different races in this race-obsessed country, it's like figuring out Chinese math. All I know is I'm glad I met Will and he says he feels the same way.

I do sometimes wonder if he'd love me if I had dark chocolate skin, short unstraightened hair, was not reed thin, not private-school educated with perfect teeth. Then you would be someone else, he says, *Aisha, stop trying to find something to point to why we shouldn't be together. You are the way you are.*

*You look the way you look. I like it, a lot, and there's nothing wrong with that.*

It's a conversation I can never really have with him. He doesn't know in his bones the legacy of what slavery did to Black people, the plantation luggage we're still carrying around just about our hair texture and skin shade. I'm café au lait with hair permed as straight as his sister's, with a twenty-three-inch waist. I totally identify as a Black woman, but on the street can be mistaken for anything from Indian to South American to East African. I'm trying to learn how to live with the fact that he won't ever get it.

I know I'm attractive, some have said beautiful, but by whose definition? At least that's what I was always taught at home when I was a little kid and Mom and I would look through magazines and I'd point out only the blondes as pretty. Mom would talk to me about why I picked one woman over another; not in a lecturing way, but very gently, she'd say, *Well, this one looks like you will look when you grow up and that one looks like Aunt Joni or Auntie Eleanor and I think they're beautiful.* Eventually I got the point.

Mom has been mute on the subject of Will's race. She asked me only once if I was ready to deal with the assumptions, the stupid comments and, in some places outside major cities, the stares. She asked me what we intended to teach our children, if we were planning to have any, about their identity . . . she's adamant about not raising them as "bi," says it's bullshit in this country. *You're either one or the other and to raise them otherwise is asking for trouble. Kids need a firm ground, not this mixed crap.* Obviously Will and I disagree with her—he more than me—and we'll deal with that when the time comes.

My dad says he just wants me to be happy, but I know he wishes I were marrying a nice young "brother" like him who pledged a Black fraternity. Everybody has his or her wishes for me. It's been a heavy burden and I just want to live and be left alone.

When Mommy got married I remember feeling like Lem was rescuing us. He was our prince. He moved us out of our two-bedroom garden apartment to a beautiful house with a backyard and swing set. I always wanted my own swing set. Mommy seemed more grateful to him than madly in love. She says she was in love with Dad but I never really believed that. I wish I could've seen her with my real father, then I would have had something to compare it to.

# CHAPTER 4

# Daddy's Rich and Mama's Good-lookin'

## *Camille*

I knew something was wrong and that I should've told someone, but I was used to figuring stuff out on my own and at eighteen, I was bound to make a few missteps. Geneva was too busy with Daddy to have time to worry about us. She sent MJ and me away to boarding school at thirteen and fourteen—we were Irish twins and in the same grade because she'd been traveling with Dad and put my brother into kindergarten when he was six. Anyway, us being at Lawrenceville freed her up to again travel. I didn't know it at the time, but she went with him to keep the hos away and make sure the money was coming in. She made sure that the often shady music-company people paid him what he was owed. In those days, I guess it's true today too, there were women of leisure who had trust funds and boredom and were always licking their lips to *sponsor* those brilliant, fine jazz musicians—the artists. The artists too lived for different experiences, believed in living life to the fullest and often that meant falling in with all kinds of different women. It was so common that Dad was weird 'cause he and Mom stayed together for fifty years and as far as I know he didn't cheat on her . . . but I digress.

Here I was starting college at Spelman—Dad thought I needed to be around some folk and Mom wanted me to become a nice colored girl—with some queasiness and weight gain. I put off going to health services because I figured it was just the new environment and being separated from MJ, who was now going to college at Princeton, down the road from Lawrenceville. (The parents had different aspirations for him.) I hadn't had much experience with Black men, there were three other than my brother at Lawrenceville and only one of them was interested in anything that looked like me, which only partially explains how I ended up losing my mind over all those fine Morehouse boys. I fell hard for one in my first semester when I saw him zooming around campus in a red Alfa Romeo convertible—with NUPE printed on the Illinois license plate. He was senior slick, dapper and from Chicago; I was a quasi-underweight insecure girl with a misshapen, out-dated Afro and glasses. A Black-White girl in Bass Weejuns and Levi's among the southern belles in heels and Diane von Furstenberg wrap dresses. I didn't even know how to dance right and was flattered and shocked by his attention, stupidly thinking if a man flirts with you and asks you out that means something. We went to places like Ponderosa and Red Lobster, which for us college students was like the Four Seasons or Bouley. He had the air of someone who'd say *Order whatever you want* like Louis "Do you want my hand to fall off" from *Lady Sings the Blues*. In my head, I'm planning our courtship. Meanwhile, he was planning how long it would take to get the panties. He'd zeroed in on my diffidence and after three dates—a movie and three dinners—he slobbered me down in his cute car before we went to his off-campus apartment; his roommate was conveniently gone for the weekend. We were watching TV or I should say he was turning the channels, looking for something that wasn't about American troops invading Grenada, frustrated, before turning on the stereo—Michael Henderson crooning "You Are My Starship." He did a little chi-chi dance as he walked toward me. I was stiffly sitting on a nubby plaid sofa.

"Dance with me." He pulled me up to him. I stood and my head reached his chest. We danced slowly, grinding it was called, he blew in my ear, licked my neck, and I wanted to get hot simply because he was the right kind of Black boy—someone who my daddy would approve of, an imagined life with someone Mom would deem appropriate. So we kept at it for a while, with me willing myself to feel something like passion, before he led me down the hall to his bedroom. I had been carrying around a pack of birth control pills that I'd gotten free during freshman orientation, but I hadn't taken any. He asked just as he was about to penetrate me if I was on the pill and I just nodded my head yes. I wanted this to be the Hollywood experience I'd been cheated out of. You know what happened next: dates, phone calls, he disappears.

Six months later I'm screaming the paint off the walls of Beth Israel, pushing out Aisha. I had just turned nineteen. I had told my parents that the Morehouse boy was the father. He was not. My brother, MJ, had come to be with me. It was his hand I almost broke, squeezing it when they refused to give me anything for the pain. There was mumbling and disapproval among the hospital staff in the delivery room so loud I could feel it. My parents stayed outside in the waiting area, my mother probably with dark shades and a scarf over her hair

and tied under her chin like Jackie O circa 1970. When the
baby was cleaned off and brought back to me, my parents
came in and they and MJ took turns holding her. We all loved
her immediately. It was the only time I can remember being
together as family and all being on the same emotional page.
But it was a strange day too—feelings of shame and pride
mixed all together, refusing to be separated. I knew I'd do my
best to raise my little girl; I'd love her fiercely and never ever
let her be on the receiving end of the kind of disdain I'd felt.
Later my brother would tell me it was that day that convinced
him to put as much distance as he could between himself and
our family. He'd make the demanded appearances during his
college breaks, less frequently during law school. After Stan-
ford, he never came back East to live, much to Geneva's disap-
pointment, because now she couldn't take him to all her social
functions to show him off—my son the big-time lawyer. Ivy
League, you know. She'd leave out the part about him being
gay. MJ hated practicing law and after five years he quit and
bought a vineyard with his lover Bill—a formerly married
man who, after he fathered two children and moved to Connecticut, realized that he was gay—and two other guys. We'd
exchange birthday cards and Christmas presents, he was a gen-
erous uncle to Aisha, but we'd let go of each other when our
lives simply became too vastly different. I know he loves me
and I'm crazy about him, but . . .

When I met Lem it had been five years since I'd let a man
near me. If the NUPE was gelato, then Lem was low-fat, no-
sugar TCBY; but sometimes, that's all you need to satisfy the
urge for something sweet. We'd go out like clockwork after
class on Wednesday night, down the way from the college, to
the diner. He was building his practice and wasn't yet ranking
in money. He was sensitive and sensible and would always ask

about my daughter, long before he'd met her. He'd listen intently whenever I went on too long about Aisha, smiling and nodding as if he were enjoying every minute of her the way I was.

When he asked me to marry him, over grilled cheese and tomato sandwiches, he presented me with a round diamond set in a yellow gold ring that was as stunningly simple as he was. I told him that I would very much like to but that I'd have to talk with Aisha just to make sure she felt as good about him as I did.

"Of course, that's the only right thing to do," he said.

Well, does that mean he's gonna be my daddy?

Only if you want him to be.

Aisha wrapped her puny arms around my neck so tight I had to loosen them to take a breath. "I guess that means you want to," I said, smiling at my five-year-old.

"When are we getting married? Can I tell Grandma? Do I get to wear a fancy dress? Can I get my hair done? Are we gonna move in his house? Does Grandpa know? What do you think he'll say?"

And we became a family.

# CHAPTER 5

# As Fine as Harry Belafonte

## Geneva

I loved Major Branch and anybody who knows me knows that. I loved my children too, but Camille obviously never believed it. Young people don't know what it's like to be with a person for a half a century; yes, I was sometimes short with Major, he was a dawdler and it often drove me crazy. He was too kind-hearted, loaning them jazz friends money all the time, often for drugs and women, that was not Christian and I didn't approve, but he could never say no. I did admire him, though. He was a talented man, with a wonderful heart and he was a better father than he was husband and that's all I'm going to say on that score. I am an old-fashioned lady, after all, and I do realize in this let-it-all-hang-out age that I'm an antique, but that's okay with me. I believe Camille's problems stemmed from trying to break too far from me, to get as far from her proper upbringing as possible—getting herself pregnant at eighteen . . . well, that's water under the bridge. Aisha is a

lovely girl, thankfully with none of her mother's rebellious-
ness, although this marrying White was not what I would've
wanted. They always take the best of us—why not take some of
those horror shows on television, the ones with the porno-
graphic clothes and hair pasted on and all that gold and mess
on their teeth? Take them.

Major certainly wouldn't have been pleased. I mean, don't
get me wrong, he wasn't prejudiced, he just preferred his own
kind, couldn't see the need to move away from our neighbor-
hoods or our institutions, he didn't want me to send Camille
and Major Junior away to boarding school (he said send them
to a Black one, they still got 'em in places like North Carolina)
but I didn't want to send my children down south during the
seventies. It hadn't changed enough for me to have felt they'd
be safe. I just didn't feel like I had a choice if I was to hold my
marriage together. I had to travel with him during the years
when he spent so much time in Europe, when things had died
in Newark and dried up just about every place else in the
States. In the seventies America was interested in disco. He had
to do his work and he had to go where it was. So I sent them to
Lawrenceville, which wasn't too far from our home in Jersey, I
had my dearest friend Trudy who lived down that way and she
would regularly check on them, and they got a superior education. What's wrong with that? Major Junior is running his
vineyard out in California, after spending years as a corporate
lawyer. He's single but happy and Camille, well, she eventually
turned out alright. I guess.

Okay, so maybe I felt like I had something to make up for,
marrying someone in the arts like Major, and maybe I
wouldn't have married him if I hadn't gotten caught. Lord
knows I was attracted to that man, at least in the beginning,
but that is not a good foundation for marriage. The Lord says

you should marry for character, not based on emotion. We know what passion did to David and Bathsheba—it blinded him and caused him to commit murder. I misbehaved something awful when I met Major. I was in my senior year, smelling myself 'cause I could see my future. I was promised to Kenneth, a boy who was going to be a dentist, and we were on our way to true Negro prosperity. I was an AKA, he was an Alpha; we were going to move to Ohio, where he was from, and he'd go into practice with his father. They'd lived as free Negroes on the other side of the Mississippi since there first ancestor took that treacherous route through the river, to the other side of freedom. I was from Georgia, from a life that was not that different from my enslaved great-grandparents'. My daddy was a sharecropper—which was just like slavery except for the whip. If my mother hadn't died having me—the midwife said I was too big—then my folks would've had a whole bunch a kids like everyone around them. I probably wouldn't have finished high school, sure enough wouldn't have gone to college.

The midwife said I cracked my mama's pelvic bone and she bled to death. Daddy took up with the Sunday-school teacher—I knew her as Mama Sadie—who helped him raise me. She was what they used to call a spinster—which was another lucky stroke for me because she was too old to have any children. I got it all—which was not much—that they had. She could read and she taught me to read when I was four years old and she and just about everybody in Wilmont, Georgia, which was the size of a high school cafeteria, thought I was some kind of genius. I don't know how Mama Sadie got it into her head that I was going to go to college—she hadn't gone past the sixth grade. Everybody around town climbed aboard her dream, adding a few pennies when they could. Daddy took on extra work at another farm and that's how I ended up at Hampton, where I met Kenneth. But after I got with Major, I prayed on it, every night, for God to make things right between us. I do believe my prayers were answered because we stayed together for fifty-one years.


Major was playing a Dizzy Gillespie rendition of "I Can't Get Started" on his trumpet when my friend Trudy and I walked into the Front Room in Newark. It was spring break at Hampton and I'd gone home with Trudy to work in her father's corner store to earn some extra money. The club was filled with smoke, and colored people (that's what we were back then) were dancing and drinking and carrying on like they were part of the leisure class. It was exciting. Trudy ordered us each a shot of bourbon. I'd never had a drink before; Mama Sadie called it the devil's potion. Trudy took out two cigarettes she'd stolen from her daddy's pack and we sat at the bar like we were Dorothy Dandridge and Diahann Carroll. Major Branch was soloing, holding that trumpet like a lady he loved, wearing a cream-colored suit, white shirt, blue and white polka-dot tie. He was sharp. Wavy-straight hair slicked back—he looked like a movie star. He was as fine as Harry Belafonte. That bourbon got to work and I felt warm and loose all over. We sat there on the red leatherette bar stools swaying back and forth, feeling fine and hep. Major was giving me the eye and I was giving it right back to him. When they took a break in the set he came over.

"How you ladies doin' this evenin'?"

Trudy and I sat and looked at each other, trying hard not to giggle and show him we were just schoolgirls.

"I ain't seen you around here before. Where you from?" he asked, looking at me but addressing both of us.

Trudy swallowed and told him she was from right here.

"You from Newark? Where'bouts?"

"Rose Terrace . . . right up the hill there."

"You my neighbor, I live on Strafford Place; and what about you, beautiful, where you from?"

I couldn't speak for fear of sounding like a country bumpkin.

"She from Georgia," Trudy said, purposely dropping the contraction.

"Georgia, huh, a Georgia peach. Well, do you have a name, or do I just call you Peaches?"

Trudy and I giggled and I finally said, "My name is Geneva."

"Well, Miss Geneva," he held out his hand, "I'm Major Branch and I'm delighted to make your acquaintance."

Trudy and I giggled some more.

"What you drinkin'? Let me get you two another one." He motioned to the bartender before we could refuse.

"Listen, Miss Geneva, I've got another set to play, but I'd like to talk to you some more. Would you stay so we can talk?"

Trudy and I looked at each other, she nodding behind him.

I blushed and said okay.

After the set and two bourbons, Major came right to me.

"So can I drive you home?"

Trudy said yes, that would be fine. I stumbled getting off the stool and he caught me by the elbow and steadied me, holding on to me as we left the club and got to his car.

The three of us got into the front seat of his Buick.

"This is a crazy car," Trudy said, skimming the dashboard with a finger.

"Thank you, Miss Trudy. The band just got a contract for an album. I treated myself."

"You got an album? Is it on the radio?" Trudy asked.

"Sho' 'nough," Major said, slipping into jazz talk that made both of us want to swoon.

He parked carefully in front of Trudy's house. We sat for a while before Trudy figured out we wanted to be alone.

"Ima be right here, on the porch, VeVe, okay? Nice meeting you, Major."

"Thank you, Miss Trudy. It was my pleasure."

She got out, careful not to slam the door, knowing her mama would be at the window if she did. She didn't dare go inside without me, so she sat on one of the metal porch chairs and waited.

Major looked at me and sighed. "If you ain't the prettiest gal I ever did see, Miss Geneva."

I looked down, embarrassed, and mumbled thank you.

"I'd really like to take you out, go to dinner and talk a little. Can we do that?"

"Um, I'm just visiting Trudy for a few days. I've got to go back to school."

"School?"

"Yes. I go to Hampton Institute, in Hampton, Virginia."

"Oh, I know it. So you a college girl, ain't that somethin'. Well, I'd really like to see you again. How about tomorrow? I pick you up, early, like five, and we'll go to JR's, have somethin' to eat. I'll have you home by seven. How's that?"

I sat, looking down into the balled napkin in my hand, thinking that I couldn't wait for tomorrow to see him again.

"Yes, that should be fine."

"Good. Five it is."

He scooted over close to me and put his finger on my chin, lifting my face to look into his deep, ebony eyes. I felt myself drowning. He leaned into me and kissed me on my lips. I was shocked and my first impulse was to pull away, but I felt the creamy effect the bourbon had on me and smelled his Murray's and before I knew it our mouths were together, tongues flicking like somebody going away to war. He moved his hand from my shoulder, down my arm and walked a finger over to touch my breast. I jumped away.

"I'm sorry, Miss Geneva, that was not appropriate. Please forgive me."

I sat, confused by a feeling that I'd never had before. I didn't want him to stop but knew that he should. With Kenneth I'd felt nothing the few times I dutifully let him kiss me but he would never dare try to feel my breast.

*Lord, what is this man doing to me?*

"You alright?"

I nodded and reached for the door handle.

"I've got to go."

"Okay. I'll see you tomorrow, then. At five."

"I'll see you at five."

"Good night, sweet peaches."

"Good night."

He waited for us to get inside and turn off the porch light before driving off.

Trudy and I held hands as we ran up the stairs in our stocking feet to her room, where her little sister was snoring in the other twin bed. We sat up half the night on her bed going over every detail from our night out.

"You let him kiss you? With his tongue?" she whispered in disbelief.

I nodded, feeling like a bad girl and secretly loving it.

"He is so fine," Trudy said. "And he really likes you."

"You think so? How do you know?"

"What, girl, he was all over you. 'Why, I think you just about the prettiest thing . . .'" Trudy said, imitating his slight baritone.

"Mmm and I'm likin' him, too."

"Girl, what you gonna do about Kenneth?"

I looked at Trudy, setting her hair on pink sponge rollers.

"Kenneth who?"

We squealed, rolling on the bed, laughing well into the night.

I thought about the respectable Negro life awaiting me. Mama Sadie would've been awfully proud. I couldn't disappoint her after all she did for me, but I had to see Mr. Major Branch again, at least one more time.

# CHAPTER 6

# The Engagement Party or
# All Over but the Shoutin'

The engagement party was held at Will's father's Manhattan apartment. It has been featured in *Architectural Digest,* okay? Enough said—no, you want details, huh. Well, you know it's one of those places that you take the elevator and it opens into the apartment. You only take that elevator if you are going to his place. The entry foyer has more square footage than the average Manhattan apartment. There's a black-and-white harlequin marble floor, wall-size antique gilt mirror, plaster urns with exotic foliage and pillars—yes, huge pillars. His ex-wife, the second wife, had been a society interior designer. She got the loft downtown.

Waiters in white gloves and careers as Broadway one-day Babies skillfully balanced trays of Moët and attitudes. Will and I stood in this area to greet our guests, many of whom we didn't know—business associates of Will's dad and granddad, his mother's painter, writer, photographer, museum friends, Camille, Lem and Grandma Geneva and a few of Grandpa's perpetually cool jazz friends—old cats who had slowed down, but were still "hittin'" as they called playing their music; Uncle MJ even flew in, despite the fight he'd had with Grandma over whether to bring his lover Bill. (Uncle MJ left Bill at home.)

You know Grandma just wanted people to see the apartment. Camille was more than a little horrified at such wealth ... *Robber barons,* I could just hear her saying to herself. *All this built on our backs.* Lem was just taking it all in: *There's nigga rich, regular rich and then there's this shit.*

In the sea of Paul Stuart–dressed men and blond-haired, Botox-faced women, there was a thin line between the regular rich and the really rich. Will's family was firmly on the beyond-regular rich, not cosmetically altered, dressed like they couldn't be bothered side. But they were all beginning to blur until a dark face entered the room with such light it almost blinded me. I dropped Will's hand and probably my mouth when I saw him or I should say felt him get off the elevator.

"Miles, my man," Will said in a way only he could say without sounding like a White boy trying to be hip.

"What's up, dawg?" They did the knuckle pump fist handshake.

"Aisha, meet the man, Miles Browning. Miles, this is my fiancée, Aisha Branch McCovney."

I just stared at him. Fortunately, he understood everything long before I did and got me to snap out of it before Will even caught on.

"Aisha, it's a pleasure," he said, firmly shaking my hand that was limp from so much hand shaking.

"You've got a great guy here. I hope you two will be very happy."

"Um, thank you and thanks for coming."

With that he walked into the party. He was wearing a cream-colored nubby jacket, probably Brioni, jeans, and brown suede loafers and some kind of scarf that he took off and handed to the person taking coats.

"So who's he?" I asked Will, trying to hide my interest.

"Oh, Miles, he's the man. He's one of Dad's friends; Dad hired him straight out of business school to work for him, and they've stayed in touch. I guess Dad was like his mentor or something."

"Hey, Aunt Pheebs," Will said, taking my hand again, pulling me toward another relative.

The stream of people continued but I could no longer focus. I felt queasy and hot, and I knew I was in trouble.

We finished up the greeting and I went in search of a large drink of water and Cedra. I needed to reality check with my best friend, whom I found talking with Will's ditz of a mother, one of a handful of women here who hadn't had anything done to her face or body. She was wearing a jumper that looked like it was from Mia Farrow's *Rosemary's Baby* days.

"Excuse us, Meredith, I need to speak to Cedra for a moment."

"Of course, sweetheart. Are you having a good time?" She was drunk already. She laughed and walked away, vodka spilling out of her highball glass.

"Cedra, have you seen that man Miles?"

"Who?"

"The Black one, the only one here who we didn't invite? The one wearing—"

"Ah, in the cream jacket? Yes. Fine."

"I'm in love."

"I know it's sweet and you're getting married."

"No, Cedra, I mean with Miles, the cream jacket."

Cedra grabbed my wrist and pulled me into a back room, an office, a sitting room, I don't know.

We sat down on a monkey-and-bamboo toile settee.

"What in the hell are you talking about? You just saw him. You're engaged to Will. Your wedding is in three months."

"I can't go through with it. I feel as if my heart stopped beating, like my breath was literally taken away, like my whole body is a nerve ending. I have to—"

"Aisha, Aisha. You don't know him. Look at me. He could be married, or gay or a serial killer or a serial lady killer— which is more likely the case."

"I don't care. I'll be his side woman or in one of his harems. I have to have him and that's that."

"Oh Jesus, what the hell . . ."

Cedra exhaled and I sat there determined and dreamy.

"Okay, can you do nothing for now? Do you think you can keep your panties on?"

I did feel moist.

"I'm going to talk to him, figure out a way to get his card. See ya."

I got up to leave and Cedra grabbed my wrist.

"Be careful, okay? Slow your roll."

I smiled at my dearest friend and went in search of my future.

Miles was talking to Will's dad when I found him.

Damn, of all people, I thought.

"Aisha, have you met my colleague Miles?"

"Yes, briefly. So do you two still work together?"

Both men chuckled.

"Work?" Garrison said. "No, we, um, confer every now and again."

"Why do I feel like there's some kind of private joke happening?"

"No, my dear, we're just 9/11 refugees, that's all. We both

left regular employment after the Trade Center thing," he added.

"Oh, so what are you doing now?" I asked Miles.

"I still do some finance, but I also have interest in a few restaurants, partnering in a hedge fund, different stuff," Miles said.

"Oh, there's my sister, I must mingle," Garrison said, and was off, thankfully.

"What restaurants? Are they in New York?"

"Sure, we own Form, Maya, and a new one that we're still trying to find a name for."

"Maya, I've been meaning to try that one. So how does that work, I mean as an investor, do you hang out at these places? Do you have like a VIP room?"

He laughed and I think it was at me.

"You are really beautiful. Will's a lucky man."

"Well, thank you." With that I zoomed in on the opening: "I'd like to see you again."

Miles took a sip of his ginger ale.

"Do you think that's a good idea?"

"It's something I have to do. How's tomorrow night?"

"I'll be at Maya."

"I'll be there at eight o'clock."

I walked away, knowing I'd spent too much time talking to him, knowing that anyone in the room who was looking at me could see that I was craving. I'd never, ever felt like this before and at this point I didn't give a damn. I knew it was all over but the shoutin'.

Shortly after Miles made the rounds of good-byes and left, I felt as if someone let all the air out of the room. I didn't want to eat, listen to toasts, stories about the Fitzhughs or Powells. I couldn't look at Will.

I can't tell you how I got through work the next day other than by taking a long lunch and busying myself on the phone, setting up potential media buys for clients. My work was the kind of job girls from good schools and with no clear ambition (read: White) ended up doing. My job was to help small stations in Upstate New York and southern New Jersey get the big advertisers to buy time on their stations. I did a lot of paperwork. I was bored to death, but it was good enough for now until I figured out how to get a job in fashion. For a lot of the girls I worked with, this was a waystation before marrying and mommying. Although I was ambitious, I didn't intend to work after I had children. I didn't know what Will expected, probably that we'd have nannies raise the kids since he was and has fond memories of them. The only person who ever took care of me other than my mother was Grandma and Miss Mabel, so I didn't see a nanny in my future.

Miles Browning gave off something—an aura, an aroma that made every other man seem like Little League.

He was drinking scotch when I met him in a draped-off room in back of Maya.

"So, this is nice," I said, looking around at the cushy seats, polished teak, claret-colored velvet drapes.

"Yeah, the decorator did a good job. We gave her the concept and she ran with it."

He motioned with his hand and I sat down across from him. He seemed so mellow, I wasn't sure he hadn't been napping before I showed up. He was wearing a white polo shirt and khakis and had a toothpick dangling from his lips.

He removed it when I sat down.

"So, Aisha, what am I to make of you?"

He looked directly at me and I'm sure with other people that stare was intimidating or something. Me, I just wanted to enter those eyes.

I sat back, put my fingers together, hands like in prayer, and put my chin on the tips on my nails.

"Well, we're going to have to do something. I feel confident that I'm not the only one feeling this intense attraction. We can do one of three things. . . ."

He smiled at me as if he were proud and nodded to indicate that he wanted me to proceed.

"We can screw our way through it and hope it's like a fever and will pass; we can ignore it and hope it goes away; or we can be together. I go home tonight, break up with Will and move in with you."

Miles, still with the smirk, acting like he wasn't surprised by anything I'd said, put his hands together and let his palms rest on his upper stomach.

"You are direct, Aisha. I like that."

I nodded and took a sip of the mojito that had been waiting for me.

"How old are you?" he asked.

"Does that matter," I said.

"Um. Yeah."

"I'm twenty-six."

He held up his glass and said, "My scotch is as old as you."

"And you're what, forty?"

"Three, forty-four in September; old enough to be your daddy."

"Not quite. Well, in the hood I guess."

"And that's home, baby. As far as you know I have a child your age."

"But you don't."

"What'd you do, Google me or something?"

Cedra had, but I didn't bother to share this.

Miles was now intrigued. He liked to be intrigued.

"Let's just say, I have special abilities."

"Oh, I have no question about that. You are somethin', ma dear."

I finished my drink and realized my stomach was gurgling.

"You want another drink, somethin' to eat?"

Before I could answer, a blond waitress/model appeared with a menu opened and handed it to me.

"My, what service," I said, looking at the menu, where I wanted to order everything.

"I'll have the rusticana salad and the pasta with shellfish."

Model/actress took the order and left.

He was grinning at me.

"Decisive. I like that."

"You're not eating?"

"Maybe later. So, you're ready to dump good ol' Will for a man you met once?"

"I did more than meet you. I felt you and I've never felt anything like this before and I believe in acting on my feelings. They've never led me astray."

"Mmm, but didn't your feelings tell you that Will was the man you wanted to spend your life with?"

I took a sip of water and acknowledged his point.

"Well, I think with Will and me, it was a decision I made with my head more than my heart."

"So you're saying you were marrying him because it seemed like the right thing to do?"

"He's a great guy, we have fun together, he loves me and I thought I loved him, but now I know I don't, at least not the way I should."

"And how do you think you should love the person you're going to marry?"

I looked at Miles, looked at my future, the man I wanted to father my unborn children.

"With everything inside you."

Miles sat up and exhaled.

"You somethin' else. So, what should I know about you, Aisha? Ima call you Ish. 'Aisha' doesn't really suit you. It's too unnatural to say, complicated in a way that you're not. Ish is direct. Do you mind?"

"My friends in high school used to call me that."

"And where was that?"

"Newark Academy, in Livingston."

"Newark Academy in Livingston," he chuckled. "Tell me it used to be in Newark."

"Yeah, a really long time ago. It sits on a few acres now, I guess that's why they moved out of the city."

"So, you went to one of dem fancy day schools, where the girls wear plaid skirts and carry around field hockey sticks?"

"A bunch of girls with blond ponytails named Emily," I added.

Miles held his glass up as if to toast me.

"So, was it good for you or did it leave you with invisible scars—Newark Academy?"

"Um, mostly it was good. My parents or I should say my mother is like a shrink and über Black so she really worked hard to keep me balanced."

"Cool. I met your mama the other night. How old is she?"

"Forty-five."

"Damn, she's young."

"Mmmmm."

"And your daddy? Lem is it?"

"Yeah, Dad's fifty-something, fifty-two, fifty-three."

"So how's your über-Black mama feelin' about you marryin' a White boy?"

"Well, I think she was kind of resigned to it, I guess. She never came out and said anything, but she didn't have to. I mean I grew up with the woman. But I also know she has a double standard for Black men marrying White women because of the numbers; she's more understanding of Black women who do."

"Oh yeah, I've heard that tired argument before. . . ."

"But it's true, the numbers of Black men graduating from college, forget professional school, is less than half the number of Black women, add in jail, unemployment, AIDS. . . ."

"Okay, okay," Miles said, holding up his hands as if to surrender.

My salad came and I inhaled it.

"So what happened after Newark Academy?"

"UVA, more blond girls named Emily and a few more Black ones."

"And was that good?"

"It was good enough, big enough to find your own group."

"Then what?"

"I considered law school, took the LSAT, got in a few law schools, decided I didn't want to go, then got a job in advertising and here I am."

"Why law school?"

"Daddy and my uncle, but my uncle hated being a lawyer."

"Daddy's a lawyer?"

"Mmm-hmm, but he's my stepdad."

Pause. Beat.

My meal arrived and I ate.

"So, you like advertising?"

"No, especially not the part that I'm in, I want to be doing something more creative. Miles, I'm starting to feel like I'm on a job interview."

"You are," and for the first time in the night he broke into a smile, revealing the most beautiful ordinary face I've ever seen. I pushed away my plate and reached across the table and covered his broad workingman's hand with mine, looked him deeply in the eyes.

"You know that this is meant to be."

He took my hand to his full lips and lightly kissed it.

"I need to get you home."

I felt like sulking, I didn't want to go home, I wanted to be with him, stay with him, but I also knew I had to act like a grown-up if I wanted to be considered seriously.

I looked at my watch and said something about how late it was.

"Nice timepiece," Miles said.

It was a Bedat with diamonds around the face and a brown crocodile band. Will had given it to me as an engagement gift. I made a note to stop wearing it. I'd have to return it. It was a beautiful watch.

"Thank you. So when do we get together again?" I said, dotting the corners of my mouth with the napkin.

"Ish, I don't know. I really have some serious thinking to do, as do you. Why don't we give this a few weeks, kind of a cool-down period before we speak again? I think . . ."

"Miles if that's what you need, fine. I don't. I've thought about this as much as I need to. I'm breaking things off with Will, regardless. So if you're more comfortable seeing me after it's done, then fine, we can do that, but I'm not hedging any bets here."

We were standing now in the private dining area and Miles looked at me with a look of trust that filled me with a power

I'd never known. He pulled me to him and kissed me, hard, enveloped me in his powerful arms, into his firm body. Our hips were pushed into to one another and I came close to coming from just that kiss. That is what desire feels like. When we stopped kissing he rested his face on the side of mine. He was breathing hard. He kissed my ears, lightly bit my earlobe. He whispered, "You know that I want you, but we've just gotta give this some time."

I nodded and said I understood.

Now for the hard part.

Thank God I hadn't moved in with Will as he had wanted me to. I went home to my empty apartment. My head was spinning and I needed to be alone with my thoughts. Why did I have to meet Miles now, why couldn't it have happened last year, before Will? This is going to break him, it's going to take away what little faith he has left in marriage and relationships, but the longer I wait to tell him, the worse it's going to be. Should I tell him it's about someone else, or that I just can't marry him?

# CHAPTER 7

# I Loves You, Porgy

## _Camille_

I untangled my Walkman from my long, graying locks as I came into the kitchen from my two-mile morning walk. The phone was ringing; it wasn't even eight o'clock yet. "I'm not ready to talk on the phone." The phone doesn't ring much and never at this time of morning. When Lem and I were together it rang day and night with people and their problems, crimes usually committed in one minute of fury. Lem rarely turned those cases over to his younger associates, preferring to drag himself out of bed to deal with the cases personally. It seemed he knew everybody in Essex County and they all wanted his personal touch when one of their own got himself into trouble and Lem being Lem couldn't say no, would head down to the police station and bail him or her out. But Lem was long gone and I lived alone. It's one thing I don't miss about being with him. It was like it must be for an obstetrician's wife.

"Yes," I answered.

"Mom?"

"Aisha? What's the matter, baby? What happened?"

Mothers know in a syllable when their children are in distress.

"Nothing horrible, I'm okay. . . ."

"Well, why do you sound like this? Did you just wake up?"

"No, I've been up all night. Do you have a minute? I need to talk."

Exhale. Run today's schedule quickly through my head. No morning meetings.

"Sure. Let me put the kettle on."

Aisha could picture her mother pouring water into the old copper kettle—she'd had it since Aisha was in kindergarten—and then pulling up a kitchen stool to the counter where a bowl of overripe bananas sat with a few tangerines.

"Okay, I'm all ears."

Aisha was crying now.

"Baby, baby, what is it, what's on your heart?"

"I can't marry Will."

Exhale. I wanted to say, *Is that all?* and then, *Hallelujah,* but I figured this was not the time.

"What happened, sweetheart? Did you have a fight?"

"No, Will doesn't even know. I . . ."

"What? What happened?"

"I . . . I've fallen in love with someone else."

Exhale.

"Well, I don't . . . Who?"

"You don't know him. His name is Miles, he was at the party—"

"Him? I met him, he's as old . . ." Take a breath, Camille.

"Mother, I know his age. It's irrelevant. I've never felt this way about anyone and I can't marry Will feeling this way about someone else."

"Well, you can, but you've decided that you don't want to."

"Mom, stop being a shrink and be my mother."

"Of course, sweetheart, I'm always your mother. I'm behind you. Whatever you decide to do, I'll support you."

Aisha let out a sigh, releasing some tension.

"I need you, Mom. Telling Will is going to be the hardest thing I've ever had to do. . . ."

"But you can and you will. You are a very strong person, Aisha. I don't think you realize how strong."

"Thank you, Mommy. I needed to hear that."

The whistle blew and I poured the hot water into my mug with lemons.

"So, do you want to tell me about this Miles or is that for another time?"

"He's wonderful. He's brilliant, he's sexy, he's funny, he's down-to-earth, he's—"

"Okay. I get the picture. Now what's he saying about all this?"

"He says we have to wait, have a cooling-down period."

"Okay. I like that. What do you know about him?"

"He's from Memphis, only child, single mother, grew up poor, went to Harvard, worked on Wall Street, was engaged once. . . ."

"So, you have a few things in common. So does he have any kids?"

"Nope. No kids. He's forty-three."

"And charming."

"Very. So, did you like him?"

I took a sip of my hot water and lemon.

"I did. We didn't talk much, but he seemed like a decent sort."

"Mommy, I'm in love. I know it sounds crazy, but I've never

felt like this before. My whole body, my being feels alive. It's like I just have to be with him."

I smiled at my daughter's words. I knew what this felt like. I'd felt this for Aisha's real father and well we know how well that worked out, but who knows maybe this will work for her. She's not me. She will have her own life.

"Baby, there's no right way to fall in love, when it happens, it happens. But you have to do right by Will. You have to sit him down and explain to him the best way you know how that you can't marry him and that it has nothing to do with him. . . ."

"Do I have to tell him about Miles?

"Is Miles the reason?"

"Well, if I hadn't met him, I would be marrying Will, but even if I don't end up with Miles, I still can't marry Will."

"I believe you should tell him the truth and Miles is part of that truth. Knowing who isn't going to alter his pain, but the sooner you tell him, the better."

I looked at the clock, it was now past nine.

"Baby girl, I gotta go to work. Call me later if you need to talk some more."

"Okay, Mom. Mom?"

"Yeah?"

"I love you."

I smiled again.

"I loves you, Porgy."

I've spent my entire adult life taking care of her and now she's twenty-six, a college graduate and gainfully employed and I am tired of taking care. I want to take care of me, have some fun, go places, have an affair, maybe get a tattoo, something crazy. I've not done anything crazy in my whole life— well if you don't count having a baby before I could vote. I don't care if she marries Will or Miles or nobody, I just want her settled so I don't have to hear that tearful-ass "Mommy, can you talk" voice ever again. Lem bored the fuck outta me for nine years, working for shit I could care less about, getting a new car every two years, thinking he's doing something for me. I like having a car until I need a new one, not because they changed the damn body type. It takes me two years to figure out all the ways the damn car works. I'm getting too old to waste my few working brain cells on meaningless shit. I want to learn Italian, how to do a headstand, how to come home from work without needing a hunk of cake, something fried and a drink—not learn gadgets. Geneva says I'm just getting like this because menopause is coming, maybe; whatever it is I don't want to be bothered with bullshit. It is one of the good things about finally getting older—you get to have yourself, of course you finally realize that all that work was the search. It's not like it's over now, hardly, but at least I know what I want and what I don't.

I trudged up the back stairs to the bathroom to shower. Pulling off my lycra T-shirt, sweatshirt, I looked at my body in the three-quarter-length mirror: breasts had sagged, belly flesh had been loosened since Aisha was born, stretch marks everywhere except my ankles. Humph . . . Did wisdom have to come with being saggy—did they have to go hand in hand? I cupped my breasts and took a side angle, wonder what I'd look like if they sat up a little higher. I sucked in my stomach and what about a little suction on this—color the gray and shoot, I'd look not a day over thirty-five, but how could I be Aisha's mother. I piled my locks onto the top of my head and liked the sexy, messy way that looked. I should color this gray, yes it's me, but I don't want to have gray hair. I'm tired of getting no attention on the street, not even the garage attendant checks me out anymore. Oh to be young and in hot love. Is it sick to envy one's daughter? Of course it is. Is it normal? Absolutely. Does that make it okay?

What would I give to have somebody hot for me and me feel the same way, when you can't wait to be with the person, that nerve-ending feeling she talked about. I never had that with Lem.

I'd expected that I would've married somebody like Daddy—a jazz musician, a mellow, sensitive man before we knew such a thing was possible. Daddy would cry when he'd read my school-made cards for Father's Day and the ones I gave him to keep in his suitcase when he went on the road. Major Branch was a great man and everybody knew it. Mother Geneva, of course, thought I should have a more proper husband and life and when I got pregnant—it shot a hole in her plan and of course she never forgave me for it. Even when I got together with Lem, a successful professional, the kind she'd wanted for me, she called him a "nappy-headed Negro from nowhere."

I realized then—what I hope my Aisha is learning—that you gotta dance to your own tune.

# CHAPTER 8

## Two Speeds

## *Aisha*

Trying to coordinate a dinner so the parents could get to know each other better had to be like figuring out the invasion of Normandy. Will's mother lives mostly in Italy; his father doesn't like almost 90 percent of the restaurants in Manhattan; Lem needs it to be in Midtown so he can get in and out (he hates the city) and Mom, well, she was the easy one—for once. Grandma was pissed that she wasn't invited. No grandparents, I told her, and she told me she was more than just a grandmother, she was my other mother. It finally happened that we agreed on having it at our home, Lem's house. Will's mother would come in the day before and be picked up and brought to the house by Will's dad. We'd pray that they were having a good day—they only have two speeds with each other—they're either the best of friends or fighting like Ike and Tina in the backseat of the limo. If they showed up with Meredith's hair in a tangle and Garrison has scratches on his face we'd know immediately which speed they were on. Thankfully that didn't happen. What did happen was an ultrapolite dinner with three couples—two of whom are divorced, the other on shaky ground.

"Aisha, I don't know what you've done to Will, but I've never seen him this happy," Meredith said to me.

"Other than the first time he sailed solo around the Sound," Garrison added.

"Lem and Camille, you've done a great job, she's just a lovely girl and we couldn't be more pleased," Meredith added.

My parents just beamed and parroted the compliment back to them.

"It is amazing that Will turned out as well as he did," Garrison said, sipping his third after dinner brandy.

"He was surrounded by screw-ups at Andover, drugs, excess, but he was just always a levelheaded kid."

"Here's to Will," Lem said.

My mom looked uncomfortable but raised her wineglass, one of many.

"I can't believe you're toasting the fact that I'm not a screw-up," Will said.

"How about a toast to Will and Aisha," Mom said, giving me the evil eye 'cause she hated pretending.

"Here here, to Will and Aisha," said Garrison.

So Will's parents got the official look-see at what I mostly come from; looked in our teeth, checked our hind parts and declared us good enough. What irony that I was prepared to toss their towheaded prince back on his trust fund. Will was a wonderful person; I was very clear about that, especially considering the ostriches that raised him, but what about that crazy, dangerously-in-love feeling? Could I live with Will, knowing that I felt it for somebody else? I was so confused.

I looked at Will, leaning forward in his chair, sitting across from Lem in front of the fireplace, who was no doubt going on in detail about his latest ambulance-chasing case, but there's Will his peaceful violet eyes nodding his head, saying to himself I know you're a pompous fool, but you're also a great guy. You're my beloved's dad. You have to love a guy like him.

I looked at Mom with her natural hair, African-print muumuu and power-to-the-people politics; she actually voted for Ralph Nader for president in the last race. My mama the race woman believes that it's up to those of us who have been the most privileged to lift up the rest of Black folk. Lem, the straight-up capitalist believes, "There is one Almighty—the dollar," and that we have to keep the dollar in the family, meaning among Black folk. One of his law partners' sons married a White woman and the father disowned him, wouldn't allow him in the house, to call, nothing. The wife has to sneak to see her grandkids.

I've bought my Romana Keveza gown—hotter than Wang. I have my borrowed and blue—Grandmother has loaned me her sapphire and diamond ring that Grandpa gave her on their twenty-fifth wedding anniversary (Grandma never gives up her jewelry). Everyone here figures the deal is done. How am I supposed to walk out on this? I know he loves me. And look at this cushion-cut rock on a diamond band. We had it designed from some of his grandmother's old pieces. Meredith thinks it's hideously ostentatious, but I don't care. She mumbled something in French when we showed everyone at the engagement party. It is a bit much, but hell, so am I. I'm sure the Bedat watch sent her over the edge, but thank God these people have good manners and keep their true thoughts to themselves.

How can I be crazy in love with a man I don't even know? With Will, I feel weirdly secure. We don't always laugh at the same things—we both acknowledged that—but he says it doesn't matter although I'm not really sure about that. When Mommy got married I remember her trying to break me out of my Cinderella-marrying-the-prince haze by explaining that you don't always get married for love, that sometimes it's bigger things like feeling safe. I guess safe wasn't enough for her. Could it be for me?

# CHAPTER 9

# Bourgie Nights

## *Camille*

My daddy was Aisha's first dad. Daddy's adoration for her was an extension of what he felt for me, further pissing Geneva off. Classic oedipal complexes, but in our case we just pretended they didn't exist. Mommy was always so cold to Daddy, belittlingly. I often wondered if she'd ever loved him. I never asked what attracted her to him; for him, he said it was love at first sight. He was playing at the old Front Room in Newark, back then Newark was a swinging place for jazz . . . there were clubs all over the city where major musicians plied their art. Mommy was visiting from Hampton, with some of her girlfriends, when Daddy spotted her and that's all I know. He said she was the prettiest, sassiest thing he'd ever seen. She was also almost a decade younger. She was twenty-one, he was thirty. She was promised to someone else, a fellow Hampton Institute student. She dropped him, Mr. Black Bourgeois, for a jazz musician—radical for its day, even today for some people. So she must have felt something for Daddy, but I can't even imagine her that way. He was big time in his day, played with Duke and Monk and Miles. He was good, the greats said he was. He worked constantly, bought her a nice house, nice cars and clothes from Saks Fifth Avenue and ours came from Best & Co., so it wasn't like they had some kind of hardscrabble more typical artist's life. Even so, I think for Geneva it wasn't quite enough. I don't know, I could be wrong, but that's the way it felt. I never could understand why she wasn't nicer to Daddy. She was so set on some vision of what we were supposed to be—this upright, Presbyterian picture-perfect family. Maybe she was like that 'cause she never knew her real mother or maybe because she came from poverty or maybe because people are just complex and some find it almost impossible to simply be content. She raised us with a kind of schizophrenia of *you're special, but not better.* We're still trying to figure out how to be that.

While they made all those "sacrifices" for MJ and me to have a better life, they forgot the things that are most important—to make us feel worthy of love. To simply be proud of us, to tell us you're wonderful, to come to our little plays at school and games, to ask about our friends—not the who-are-their-people kinds of questions, but why do you like so-and-so. Children need help to understand themselves, to value themselves and their opinions. Now at forty-five I'm stuck trying to figure out who the hell I am—Papa was rich (as in nigga rich) and Mama was good-lookin' and what the hell did that give me; that and a token will get me downtown.

While they were stompin' at the Savoy in London I was trying to see what love felt like at Lawrenceville.

When MJ and I arrived on the bucolic Lawrenceville campus with our parents in tow, we walked ahead of them, embarrassed by their perfect Sunday-best outfits—Geneva in her yellow wool bouclé suit with the huge fox collar and Dad in his brown-and-white checked silk sports jacket and wraparound Ray-Bans. He actually looked cool—he always did to me—but we couldn't single Mom out, so we pretended to be repelled by them both. My brother and I played it cool together, trying hard not to seem overly impressed, although we completely were, we'd later admit to each other. The place was out of a storybook, complete with the ivy-covered buildings, kids walking around carrying lacrosse sticks, and golden retrievers with bandannas around their necks. Even the notable Newark Academy, where I'd practically sold my kidneys to send Aisha, looked like a dump in comparison. After a week of getting-to-know-you activities, we settled into our work—which was tougher than any college. We worked hard, but we had fun, and remember this was the seventies and the race piece was much cooler than it is now. We really did think it was possible to all be brothers—many of us did anyway. MJ was soon swept up into sports and fraternal-type activities. I only saw him at Sunday supper, where we'd catch each other up. He became a big man on campus—inevitable for a good-looking, agile Black boy. I inherited a few specks of spillover glory by being his sister. Basically we did what we'd been trained to do—we made the best of our Lawrenceville years. I was a slightly above average student and MJ, being the oldest, was slightly above me. He certainly worked harder. We were soldiers, after all, so we soldiered on in our parents' persistent absence.

Adam was a scholarship student only because, he said, his father had died and his mother was a hippie. They were educated and broke and Adam applied as an emancipated adult. Folks at Lawrenceville expected MJ and me to be on the dole—we weren't, Adam was. He did plenty to help them in that assumption. We met in study hall—another jock sniffer

who just wanted to be near MJ and figured studying with me
was like getting to know MJ. Studying led to going for burgers
and milk shakes, which ended up with us actually getting to
know each other. We quietly dated and eventually began having sex. Neither of us knew what the hell we were doing and
for most of the four semesters we were together, did nothing
more than lots of talking and rubbing bodies in our clothes.
He was much more cautious and conservative about having
sex than me. He had something to prove to his embarrassed,
still-hung-over-from Woodstock mom. His plan was to go into
business and become rich. He'd hated living the way they had,
cushions on the floor, batik fabrics as curtains and upholstery.
He hated the vegetarian diet, the steady stream of people
bunking on the sofa, but more than anything he hated people
asking him: *What are you anyway?* Most Black people recognized what his racial makeup was, but too many White folks
would question it. His way of dealing, I think in retrospect,
was to build an empire, become the capitalistic striver his
mother tried to raise him not to be, and everything would be
good. I knew Adam was a sensitive, loving man and we'd
promised to stay in touch from our colleges—he'd be all the
way up in New Hampshire, at Dartmouth, and I down at Spelman in Atlanta. Although most high school romances don't
make it past freshman year, I'd planned that we'd be the exception. What I hadn't planned on was how it felt to be around all
those fabulous Black folks for the first time in my life. As I
said, I just lost my mind. Adam had a slight build, wavy light
brown hair and didn't think of himself as attractive. He was
way too insecure to pursue me after his cards and calls went
unanswered for longer and longer intervals. He'd had some
attention from the girls at school, but I knew that in college,
once he grew into his body more, the girls would start to

notice him and I figured he'd be better off with some Muffy who could help him get into the country club. We lost touch after I left school and I never told him about what we'd made.


I sit while my client talks about her abusive father. He used to beat her with a brass belt buckle, she still has some of the dark keloid scars on her arms; he was mean like Mr.—— in *The Color Purple*, like the kind of men my mother used to talk about in the south whose spirits were so destroyed from years of pent-up rage at being treated like the gum on society's shoe. Hearing my mother's stories about growing up in the south I couldn't help wonder how much of that rage she'd experienced personally, but I never had the heart to ask. Since I've been doing this job, I've heard the story so often of the violent, alcoholic father that I oftentimes think my own sweet-natured, triumphant father was a fantasy. Am I less part of the culture because I didn't have an abusive or absent father? My clients know very little about my personal life, which is how I designed it, the only way my help works, but I can't be completely removed from them as my Eurocentric training would have it. They know that I was a single, teenage mother and they think that helps me to understand their struggles more. It does. They don't know the material privilege I grew up with and sometimes I feel guilty for keeping that part of me hidden, but I just can't open it to them and often don't open it for discussion to myself. Having had nice things doesn't immune one from pain, but in a million years, they couldn't be convinced. But even with me having been a mother at nineteen, having done the night shift at the post office to pay for college, my life was an island breeze in comparison. "Shoot, at least you had somebody to watch Aisha, you ain't have to worry 'bout her gettin' abused and shit. My baby got took from me 'cause I left her wit my girlfriend and the fool who was livin' wit her abused my baby. She was only two years old, okay. What kind of sick muthafucka would do some shit like that, you tell me, Dr. Camille? Who?"

My clients have served prison terms—always related to some man, shooting him for sexually abusing their kid or for beating them or holding drugs or selling drugs for him. Their pain is unknowable by most people and they just want what most people in this country have, a safe clean place to live and a better chance for their kids. Simple.

Although I work long hours, it's never enough. There are always so many broken lives that just need glue. By the time I get home, I have a drink, try not to smoke a cigarette, instead I'll have some cake, some Popeye's I picked up on the way home and pass out only to wake up and start the whole thing all over again. I've thought about going for my doctorate—but when would I have the time? They call me doctor because they think I am and the certification is meaningless in their world.

# CHAPTER 10

# What Kind of Name Is Aisha?

## *Aisha*

After the parents' gathering at Lem's, I knew I had to end things with Will. The wedding had taken on that runaway-train quality and I knew that if I didn't end it now, there would be no stopping things. I called Will and said that we should meet, that I had to talk. I got to Café con Leche first, looked around and was glad that it wasn't crowded. The usual types were there—a group of Banana Republic–attired moms with their toddlers, a few guys with their laptops; one Norah Jones I'm-a-poet chronicling her feelings on a legal pad. I saw Will through the window, his bouncy walk made him seem younger than twenty-seven, and I think, How could I tell him? How could I? He looked at me with his puppy trusting eyes filled with loved.

"Hey, sorry I'm late." He kissed me.

"I ordered you a decaf."

"Oh good, thanks. So what's up, you sounded upset on the phone?"

He sat, blowing into his hands, face still red from the cold.

"I, um, I . . ."

The waitress brought his coffee and asked him if he wanted anything else.

"No, I'm cool for now, thanks."

"You sure you're alright? You look a little tense."

"I haven't been sleeping well."

"Oh boy, are the wedding jitters starting already?"

"You know me, I'm precocious."

"Oh, speaking of wedding, my mom wants to take you to lunch."

My look gave me away: I'd rather have gone in for a root canal.

"It's about some standard family stuff . . . you know, when a Powell heir marries . . ."

"So there's cash on her side too?"

Will nodded.

"A lot?"

Another nod.

"More than the Fitzhugh side?"

"A lot."

"Oh, Will."

"I know."

"I thought she married up. So, you're like a double-rich kid. You're really, really rich."

"Aisha, you know this doesn't have anything to do with me or you for that matter. We can give it all away. Would that make you happy?"

"Um, no. It would make me happy to not have to have lunch with your mother."

"I'm afraid there's nothing I can do about that. How about we make it breakfast, that way it won't drag on."

"That's cute. I'll meet her for lunch," I heard myself say, digging in even deeper.

Meredith Elizabeth Powell Fitzhugh Martin was a vision in a blue sweatshirt, a tan blazer that looked like something her cats used as a scratching post, khakis and Tretorns when we met for lunch at her neighborhood spot, La Goule. My Luciano Barbera suede jacket was wasted on her. La Goule is a staple, Madison Avenue bistro where women tote Hermes Birken bags and dress in cashmere shawls, turtlenecks, slacks, south sea pearls and Tod's loafers—restrained elegance and faces so tight you couldn't get an expression from them if you farted. But Meredith stood out as true old money, rejecting the status-conferring accoutrements of the more ostentatious newer arrivals. She didn't need any of it.

I purposely arrived early. The maitre d' had been expecting me and led me to a choice window table. I sipped a seltzer, knowing that I would have to drink something alcoholic with Meredith.

She arrived slightly later than our appointed time and apologized for the five minutes I'd had to wait.

"I couldn't find a place to put my bike, silly flower pots. This city doesn't have enough bike racks or meters."

We kissed Euro-style and she sat down. A whiff of something she'd been wearing since Miss Porter's filled our space.

"Aisha dear, good to see you."

"Yes, thanks for inviting me."

She fingered the silverware, rearranging it the way she liked it.

"Your name is lovely. What kind of name is Aisha?"

I wanna say to her that I was aware that I seem like more of an Ashley or Amanda but my mother saddled me with a name that would force me to deal with my race and class and I've resented her for it for most of my life. I know changing it would hurt her and tell her too much about my real feelings, so I've kept them to myself and tried to learn to somehow become Aisha, a Black-White girl with a Black-Black name. I want to tell her I know it's a *Daily News* name, but I don't.

"Oh, you know, it's one of those seventies names, like Sunflower, but only Black."

She smiled a tight little confused smile and I wasn't sure if it was because she didn't know what I meant or was uncomfortable at my mentioning race.

"I see," she said and moved on. "Now, dear, since you're marrying my son, I think we need to get to know each other a little, don't you?"

The waiter brought her a clear martini with an onion and lingered as she took a sip.

"Perfect," she said without looking at him.

"Aisha dear, have something, what is that seltzer water? How about a nice whiskey sour?"

"I'll have a glass of chardonnay. I have to go back to work."

"Of course. Now, I don't know how much Will has told you about our family. . . ."

"I know he has a sister who's studying in India, and that you and his father divorced when he was fourteen."

"Yes, that's right. Emma is in Bangladesh, Bombay, some godforsaken place, getting a post-doc in God knows what, I don't why, but . . . no, I mean about our, how do I say, background."

"Will hasn't told me much." I wanted to say, *What is there to tell, other than you're stupid phat rich.*

She swirled her martini and seemed happier with each sip.

"Well, what about your family? I so enjoyed the other night.

The home is lovely. And your grandmother, I missed seeing her again."

"Believe me, she wanted to be there. . . ."

"What a lovely woman, and I understand that your grandfather was a quite a musician, jazz, was it?"

"Yes. He played the trumpet."

"Garrison says he was quite important in that realm."

"Yes, he was considered a musician's musician."

"And your mother is a social worker?"

"Yes, she runs a center for needy families."

"That's wonderful. We talked about getting some of our boards together on some fund-raising efforts."

"That would be great. They always need money."

"And what about your father, dear? I understand Camille raised you on her own before she married Lemuel, but do you see your," she paused, clearly struggling for the right word to describe him and finally gave up and said, "your dad?"

For the first time during my relationship with Will, I felt what they'd being doing all along: looking at me through a microscope. I hadn't dealt with this bullshit question about my real father in as long as I can remember. Lem was the father I had and that was all anybody needed to know. *How dare she,* I wanted to say, but I restrained myself, easy to do in a place like this.

"Actually, I don't. Lem is my father."

I felt myself grinding my teeth and looked Meredith deep into her paler version of Will's eyes. She had the good sense to back off.

"Of course, dear, and he's lovely."

The waiter came back just in time to take my order, because apparently Meredith ate the same thing every time.

She explained to me that she "couldn't be bothered" with looking at a menu, coming up with new things to eat. She ate the same thing on the same day, every week, chicken cutlets today—it's Thursday.

We continued our lunch in polite Upper East Side custom, words dancing about, saying nothing.

"So," she said, as we were eating our sorbet, "I should give you what I came here for, well, one of the reasons."

She handed me a thick document.

"What's this?"

"Oh, yes, Aisha dear. The reason for our little lunch: it's a prenuptial agreement. Standard stuff; it's kind of like a family tradition, you could say. . . ."

"Oh, may I—"

"Oh, you can just sign it and I'll take it back with me, give it to John, our lawyer, be done with it."

"Um, I think I'd like to read it over, before I sign it, you know, just so I know what I'm putting my name on."

"Oh, of course, Aisha, smart girl like you, of course. Take it, look it over. It's fine."

Now I really knew I was in a different country: a prenuptial, a family tradition, that's how much money these folks had and had to protect, especially from some Black girl whose real daddy nobody knew anything about. I was surprised they hadn't kidnapped Will to keep him from marrying me. Guess they were too sophisticated for that—they'd just make him think that they supported it—and factor in the inevitable divorce. No sense in having him turn on them.

I folded the twenty-some-odd papers into my purse. Meredith signed the check and I told her I had to get back to work.

I walked down Madison with this thing in my purse, not knowing what to do with it.

By the time I got back to my office, the ten-block walk and the March air had cleared my head.

# CHAPTER 11
# Pimp-slap Will

## *Aisha*

I got back to work, picked up the phone, dialed Will's extension and hung up.

I couldn't, not yet. I called Cedra.

"What's up, you?"

"Nothin', just avoiding work . . . Will . . . what're you . . . ?"

"I'm working on a model. I gotta go into a meeting in about five. You okay?"

"No."

"Hey, what happened at the lunch with Will's mom?"

"She wants me to sign a pre-nup."

"Oh. Is that's all?"

"Whaddya mean, is that all. I don't want to sign shit."

"Oh, darling, no you didn't. You're in the big leagues now and that's how they do it. You sign or you don't marry the prince."

"Well . . ."

I could hear someone talking to Cedra in the background.

"Sorry, babe, I gotta hop. I'll call you later."

*Click.*

I looked at the phone. No, she didn't just hang up. I admired and envied Cedra's career commitment; I do sometimes wonder if my girl's heart is not frozen, though. Nothing else really mattered to Cedra. It's true what they say about opposites, even in friendship. We couldn't be more different. Cedra is all mental, no interest in feelings, could care less about gossip although she did Google Miles and seem very interested in tracking all the models/fill-in-the-blanks that he'd dated.

"He is a majordomo, major Wall Street player and a player-player," she'd concluded after her Google search.

"Are you telling me that as encouragement or as a warning?"

"Just be careful, that's all. He is very big league."

"Thanks for your concern, but I think I can handle this," although I hadn't really felt that she was concerned about me.

When we were little, Cedra was the most fun to hang with. Our imaginations seemed so completely in sync. We'd act out books—dress up like *The Lion, the Witch and the Wardrobe,* we always took our Jack and Jill activities very seriously; when the other kids were pouting and complaining that their mothers made them come, we would show up for the Kwanzaa celebration with our heads and bodies draped in old curtains mimicking African dress; for a commemoration of Harriet Tubman, we'd become Harriet, skipping weekly hair-straightening appointments to wear our hair natural like the leader of the Underground Railroad. But when Cedra's parents split up, around the time we were turning thirteen, she changed. Her fun imaginative self just seemed to gradually disappear. She became obsessed with getting all *A*s in high school, getting into the college with the best architecture department and the top master's program. She said she'd never wanted to be dependent on anybody, financially or emotionally after seeing how her father had left her mother for her mother's best friend, a sorority sister from their college days at Fisk. He married the friend but the marriage lasted, as my grandmother would say, about as long as the reception. Now her dad only dates women who are practically our age. She says she hates her dad. I know that's not true, but she's so angry at him, it's something almost irrational and she doesn't see how she's been consumed by her anger toward him.

As an architect she has that cool spare look about her, all her clothes are black or beige or white and cotton, silk or wool. She wears her hair short and natural and wears a funky version of Buddy Holly eyeglasses that all architects seem to own. She's constantly hit on by gay women, but she isn't gay, although she says it would make life easier since she thinks women are so much better than men and a lot of the women she meets through work are gay: *I'm just not into eating pussy, although I would be open to receiving.*

I picked up the phone again to call Will.

"Hey," he answered, sounding distracted.

"You busy?"

"Um, yeah, uh, hang on."

He put the phone down. I looked at my nails, it was time for a manicure. He got back on the phone.

"Hey, how'd it go with my mom?"

"She wants me to sign a pre-nup. You knew that's what she wanted, didn't you?"

"Um, yeah. I thought you knew too; what other kinds of papers could I have meant?"

I felt stupid and hated it.

"Will, don't talk to me like that; not everyone grew up with a fucking trust fund, some people—"

"Ash, look, I can hear that you're upset. I should've said something. . . ."

"Yes, you should have."

"My bad. Look, this is stressful—"

"Don't even try to weasel out by telling me how stressed you are."

"Babe—"

"And don't Babe me. You listen to me, Will."

"Awright."

"Your mother should not have been the one to present it to me—like I'm some kinda gold digger—it should've come from you. I had no idea your ass was fucking loaded, okay? And from where I sit, how loaded is irrelevant. I grew up with every fucking thing I thought I wanted, so I don't feel like I'm some poor, deprived Black girl, okay?—and you need to let your fucking parents know that—okay?"

Will was silent. He'd never felt my wrath before.

"And she starts with the question about my name, 'just what kind of name is Aisha,' like just what ghetto are you from exactly, and she asked about my father, like who's your real dad and all that shit. Why didn't you tell them that I don't know where my father is?"

By now I was yelling and crying.

Will exhaled loudly.

"I'm sorry, babe. I'm so sorry. I just . . . I guess I didn't know how to tell them something like that. Look, I'm coming down; let's take a walk."

"I don't want to go for a fucking walk, plus I've got get some releases done that are due in"—I looked at the clock and I had less than an hour—"I have to go."

I hung up and turned to my computer.

I hated this job.

As I finished typing up time-slot agreements, Will shows up in my doorway.

"You finished?"

I took what felt like the first breath all day and nodded.

"Let's go grab a coffee."

"Forget the coffee. I need a drink."

"Uh, Ash, it's only four o'clock."

"I know, but I can leave. I'm done for the day."

"Okay, but I'm not. I'll go with you but I gotta come back at some point."

I changed out of my office loafers and pulled on my high-heeled boots. He helped me with my jacket and I turned off my desk light, letting everyone know I was gone for the day.

"I wanna show you something."

We went to the New York Public Library.

"I don't think they have cocktails here," I said, looking around the massive main room. It was the main reading area of the library. He pulled me over to a plaque on the wall: THE POWELL ROOM, 1912, REED BROWN POWELL.

"A relative?"

"My great-grandfather."

I looked up at the massive ceiling fresco and felt tiny and slightly queasy.

"You wanna see something else?"

I walked over to a bench.

"So, your great-grandfather, what, donated the money to build this?"

"Basically, yeah. He had the whole thing commissioned, picked the artist, designer, architect, whatever they were back then and paid for it."

I said, clicking my heel on the grand marble, "Wonder how much the flooring cost."

"Come on. I wanna show you something else."

He pulled me from my seat and we walked out to Fifth Avenue.

"Can you walk in those?" he said.

"Where are we going?"

"Grand Central Station."

"What're we going there for?"

"More introductions to the Powells."

"I don't know how much more I can take," I said as I trotted alongside him in my Marni thigh-highs.

We got there and stood for a rare moment, just looking up at the massive structure.

"Don't tell me he donated this too."

"No, my paternal grandfather paid to have it restored. My maternal great-great had it built."

"Why are you doing this now?"

"I need for you to see. I was trying to keep it from you, 'cause it doesn't matter to me. I forget the magnitude, 'cause I grew up knowing all this, but you're just coming into it. You need to see it, to help you understand where they're coming from."

"And what about where you're coming from?"

I looked around, feeling like I was seeing this train station, this institution, for the first time ever.

"You want to see more?"

I would only admit this to my best friend, no not even her, but was intrigued by just how much moolah we're talking about. *Am I being a fool for throwing away a life most people never even dared imagine for a man I didn't know? Will loved me and we could probably be really happy together.* I needed to sit.

"No, I think I've seen enough for now."

"Good, let's go get that drink."

We walked over to a hotel that catered to the fashion-magazine folk.

I ordered a blue martini. Will had a beer.

"Ash, I hope you understand how little all this means to me. I showed you the room so that you'd understand who and what you're dealing with. My mother came from all that and is probably one of the most unhappy people I've ever met, my dad, too, although he's not all that unhappy. It means nothing. I want a normal life, with a normal woman and a house and kids who go to school and come home every day. I really do want to marry you and if you don't want to sign those papers, then don't sign them."

"What happens if I don't?"

"I'm not sure, but I imagine it means I'm cut off. The idea is just protection; they're keeping the money in the family. . . ."

"You make it sound so logical."

"In a way it is. It's the only way I know."

"I just hate the idea of getting married and thinking about getting divorced."

"I know, but we don't have to think about it. It doesn't have to mean anything, or if there's something in it that you don't like we can make them change it."

He was so damn earnest, but with parents like his, how could he be for real?

We drank in silence. Will looked distracted. I knew he was already back at work thinking about his copy for the pro bono charter-school work that he had made the firm take on.

I was off thinking about my real father, something I hadn't done in years.

# CHAPTER 12

# The Azaleas Were in Bloom

## *Geneva*

My life is so simple and quiet now, probably more than most widows' since Major and I had had such an active life. He lived as a musician, the way he wanted and died that way too. He was hardheaded, wouldn't see the doctor regularly so he didn't know that he had so many blocked heart valves. He had a heart attack in bed late one morning (all his mornings were late since he was usually up late playing the clubs). I was right here at my kitchen table, having my second cup of tea, getting his breakfast together—he always ate light when he got up. He liked broiled grapefruit, a little toast and a cup of strong coffee. It was just past eleven-thirty, I remember because I thought, Well, that's strange, he wasn't out that late last night. Usually I'd hear his footsteps shuffling down the hall around eleven even. I sat some more, enjoying my tea, looking out over my garden, noticing that my azaleas were in bloom. You had to enjoy the azaleas 'cause the blooms are so short-lived.

Anyway, I sat thinking about my flowers, remembering how I use to have Aisha out there in my garden with me. How she loved to help me weed and water. She was always a fast learner, remembering the names of all the different annuals. She was away at college, down in Virginia. I missed her so. When she did come home on breaks, she'd stay half with Camille and the other half with Major and me. Camille didn't like it, but she had the good sense not to complain. Aisha and I would have girls' night where we'd wear our pajamas, eat popcorn and watch TV in my bed. She always noticed the little things that I thought were important, like fresh-smelling sheets and smooth blankets, the small cut-crystal vase of roses on my bed stand. My kids could care less, they'd probably sleep on burlap if I'd let them and they never noticed the flowers. Anyway, when it got to be around eleven forty-five I went to the hall and called Major. He didn't answer. I thought he was probably in the bathroom so I went back to my tea and waited a few more minutes, saw a cardinal in the backyard magnolia tree, watched the squirrels dig for grubs. When he didn't come by noon, I went after him. When I walked into the bedroom and saw him lying on his back with his mouth open, and I just knew he was gone. Even though he looked like he was sleeping, there was a feeling in the room that something had happened, something or someone had been here and taken my Major away from this life as we know it. I stood in the doorway, taking some deep breaths before going to him, sitting on his side of the bed and putting my hand on his face. He was cool and hard and still as handsome as he was the first time I saw him at the Front Room nightclub in downtown Newark. I held his hand and said a prayer. You don't quite know what to do when you lose a person that's been with you for more than fifty years. There are no words. After a while I got up and called

Whigham's to come and get the body. They would know what to do from there. I called Camille and MJ and then I called Trudy, who was then living in Arizona. "I'm on my way," was all she said. It was all she had to say. I knew I'd get through this now because Trudy had been with me even longer than Major. She was my dearest friend. Camille showed up before the funeral parlor still half dressed in her nightclothes, and tried to hold herself together for my sake, but she was broke down. Trudy arrived that night; MJ arrived the next day as did Aisha and we were all in the house together for the next week, just taking care of each other. It was the last time I had a full house. I've been here alone ever since.

Now I go to the church, talk to Trudy on the phone, plan our annual trip—this year we're going to back to Vegas—do my gardening, a little canning. Aisha and I still talk about doing girls' nights, but she's so busy we haven't done it in a long time. I don't like to nag her. She's young and has so much going on, especially now with the wedding plans and all. Now we talk about what was on Oprah which she knows I make a point to watch every day. She sometimes catches it late at night when she can't sleep and she'll call me the next day from work to talk about it. Mostly I know she's just checking up on me. I don't mind. I love hearing from my girl. The last time she called we talked about a horror of a show Oprah had on about these young girls somewhere in Africa who couldn't control their waste and urine and just smelled something awful. They became social outcasts and were put away to live alone in hut. There was this Australian woman doctor who does operations on the girls for free, sews up their bladders, takes care of them and sends them back to their villages with a new dress and a new life. Aisha and I both were just overwhelmed by this story. She said she wanted to do something, told me that she'd already sent money. The operations cost four hundred fifty dollars and Aisha had set up a plan to pay thirty-five dollars a month for an operation. I told her that was the right thing to do and that I was proud of her. I was going to put that African hospital on our women's missionary-club list for a donation. Aisha is a good girl. She always asks about Aunt Trudy—that's what all my kids call Trudy—and I told her Trudy hadn't been feeling too well. We'd even had to postpone our trip to Vegas. I didn't really want to go anyhow, but Trudy loves to play those slot machines. She could sit there for hours putting money into that silly thing. I always ask Aisha about the wedding and about Will and she sounds happy enough and says things are right on track.

I never told her what I thought about her marrying Will, well, because she'd never asked me. I don't know what I'd say if she did. I'd die before I'd hurt my little girl's feelings, but I never was too crazy about the idea. There are all kinds of fine-looking colored, I mean, Black boys doing things. I see them on TV and sometimes when I go into the city to the theater. I don't know why she can't find one of them.

# CHAPTER 13

# Take Your Fast Car and Keep on Drivin'

## *Camille*

I pour myself a third glass of champagne. I sure have made up for all those years I didn't drink while I was busting my ass raising Aisha. I never drank, never smoked weed (after I left Lawrenceville), never went to clubs, dressed like a skank or flirted with men. I had to be responsible. Someone was relying on me. During the five years I worked at night and went to school during the day, I slept from three P.M. to six P.M. while Aisha was in after-school. I got my master's while working full-time. By the time I married Lem, I was exhausted. It was the first time I let someone share the financial load because I'd refused to take any money from my parents. I had something to prove and I was going to even if it killed me, which it damn near did. I'd finally given in to what my mother had wanted for me—Negro respectability. Lem, Aisha and I moved into our lovely home in a good town and for a while everything was fine—till she was about twelve and started acting a fool and Lem and I clashed over what to do about her misbehaving. He didn't believe in spanking or even any real punishment. "Let her be, she's a princess," he'd say—his own fantasy, again, a version of Negro respectability. I wasn't feeling that or him. Lem was getting on my nerves and boring me and I'd rather be beaten than bored. After seven years we divorced and I bought this very frame house in a neighborhood that was being gentrified, it tipped backward and now it's simply the hood. I kept Aisha in the private school I couldn't afford. Even though Lem offered to continue to pay her tuition, I refused and got her in on a scholarship for underserved children because we lived where we did and I had social-worker connections. I did let him take her shopping twice a year—she needed to not look underserved at Newark Academy. He was happy to do it, since this was how Lem showed his love, through buying things. He never understood why he couldn't just buy stuff for me and make me happy. I never cared about things—jewelry or clothes or cars, none of that was ever important to me. Maybe 'cause I'd grown up with it; maybe because it was so damn important to Geneva. Aisha's felt underserved in some deep way all her life, but again, she doesn't know it. She thinks all that craving for designer this and high-end that is just because she has such great taste. You can have great taste and find stuff at Target. She's been trying to use possessions as salve for her entire life and I wonder how long it'll work. She's always been a trooper for me, for her grandma, all of us who she saw doing all we could so she wouldn't feel like the poor little Black girl who doesn't know her real daddy.

I didn't even know I was pregnant initially. I was at Spelman—I was a kid and acted like one. Wishing the whole thing away . . .

My Kappa had acted like a complete ass when I told him and then I backtracked and realized it wasn't him after all—at the time it was easier to just not say a word.

I promised myself that I'd make June Cleaver look like Stella Dallas. I would be Mother of the damn Year. For the most part, if I have to say so myself, I did. Aisha had a wonderful childhood and is an intelligent, thoughtful, ambitious girl, with a great sense of compassion and style, albeit a little too high end for my taste or her budget. I did do a good job. Sometimes I worry that maybe I did too good.

There's a fire blazing in the fireplace, I've got my favorite CDs on, Tracy Chapman is belting out "Fast Car" and I'm celebrating Friday. Aisha called to say she's coming over and I'm trying to savor this moment before she shows up. I live alone, have my work and peace of mind and my baby is getting married, about to become somebody else's problem. I know what she wants to talk about. She's coming over on a Friday night, forgoing her friends and fancy bars to come see her mama, says she just wants to hang out, but I know her better than she knows herself: this thing is too heavy on her little mind. But right at this moment, life is perfection. I wish I could bottle it. *Somebody's got to take care of him, so I quit school and that's what I did. . . .*

I hear Aisha putting her key in; she seems startled to see me in the living room, where I'm stretched out on floor cushions and pillows, the only light coming from the fire.

"Hey, Ma. You looking comfy."

"I am, dahlin'. Come here and give Mama a kiss."

She's so beautiful, she's breathtaking. I never do get used to it. She takes off her winter-white coat and hangs it on the coat rack, sits on the window seat and unzips her lovely cream suede boots.

"Oh boy, you pulled out the Tracy Chapman?"

"It's still great."

"Yes, Mother."

"Did you take the bus out?"

"No, I took a car service from work."

"I was wondering how the hell you walk in those boots. You want some champagne? It's not cheap."

Aisha came over and took the bottle out of its bucket.

"Not bad," she said, looking at the label.

"You are such a snob . . . where did you come from?" I cry in mock horror.

She pours herself a glass and joins me on the floor.

"So, how're you feeling, Mom?" she said, rubbing my leg.

"I'm great," I say, eyeing her suspiciously, "But I know you didn't come out here to talk about me. What's happening?"

"Oh, nothing."

"Mmm." I eye her.

"How's work?"

"The same."

"How's Will?"

"Confused."

"Oh?"

After she drinks her first glass and pours another for us both, finishing the bottle, she tells me that she had lunch with Will's mother yesterday.

"They want me to sign a pre-nup."

"Whaaaaa? . . . Well, I guess we should've expected that. How rich are they?"

"Her side's even richer than the father's. Will took me on a little tour of my family's Manhattan—"

"Really?" I said, sitting up so I didn't miss hearing anything.

"Mmm-hmm."

She told me about the room at the library and Grand Central Station.

"And you didn't know?"

"No idea. I knew they were rich, but they're like Rockefeller rich."

"No. So, what are you going to do?"

"I don't know. I haven't decided what to do about the pre-nup."

I looked at my little girl with her perfect little almond eyes and sweet pouty lips and wanted to make her decision for her, but I knew she'd have to figure it out on her own.

"I haven't talked to Miles."

"And? I thought that was the agreement."

"It is, but I want to . . . especially after this . . ."

"You want my advice or you just want me to listen?"

She looked at me and nodded reluctantly.

"Don't call him. It'll just confuse things even more. Let all this stuff with Will sort out."

"What is wrong with me? Why am even I thinking about Miles when I have Will right here in my hand?"

"I don't know, maybe something's telling you he's not so in your hand or . . ."

"What're you trying to say, Mom?"

"Well, what do you think about him not telling you about the pre-nup before the lunch with Meredith?"

"Oh, I already let him have it about that. That was crazy."

I nodded, believing that maybe she had things under control.

"You know we never talk about the elephant in the room," Aisha blurted out.

*I always hoped for better, you'd get a job and I'd get promoted.*

I was feeling good listening to Tracy croon, and I didn't want to go heavy.

"Do we have to now?"

"It seems like as good a time as any."

"Are you staying the night?"

"Yeah. I don't feel like going back out into the cold."

"Well, glad I could provide warm shelter."

"You know what I mean, Ma. Of course I wanna hang with you."

"That's better, dammit."

"So, Will's White."

"*What?* You're kidding. I thought dey was just pale."

"Stop it, Ma."

I sat up, breathed deeply and got into a lotus position.

"Well, what do you want me to say?"

"I know you have some kind of feelings about that and I know you've been holding back from me. I don't want you to do that."

"Mmm, so you want me to tell you what I think about you being with Will, a White guy?"

"Not just being with him, Mom, marrying him."

"Well, it's not clear that this marriage is actually going to happen," I chuckle, admittedly in bad taste.

"Ma! Stop! We're engaged and you and I, who talk about everything, haven't talked about this and it's stupid and we need to stop."

"Okay. You're absolutely right. I think Will's a wonderful guy. . . ."

"Yeah, yeah—"

"Just hold on. And I think if he were Black I'd be thanking God on my knees every night. I do think there will be issues, not necessarily problems you can't solve, but you'll have problems. You come from such different places, the race piece being just one difference."

"You're talking about the money?"

"I'm talking about what comes with it, sweetheart. The very rich really are different. The divorces, the moving around, even boarding school, and those are just surface things."

"Well, you went to boarding school . . . and my parents are divorced."

"So maybe I know a little bit about it. Why do you think I didn't send you? That should tell you something."

"So you're saying you have more problems about his money than his race? Come on, Ma."

"I'm not saying that, but I know that there are the rare White folks who are capable of viewing us as equals and maybe you've got yourself one in Will."

Aisha was quiet for a second. She was so my daughter. Like a little amateur shrink, I could smell her gears turning.

"Okay, so that's what you think. How do you feel about it?"

"Oh God, Aisha. You're blowing my high. I don't want to have this conversation right now. Is that alright with you? Can't we do it another time?"

"Yes, after you answer the question."

"Okay, you wanna know how I *feel*, I feel like I did something wrong, like I missed a step. Like maybe I shouldn't have sent you to Newark Academy or I should've made you go to Howard or . . ."

"Like a failure as a mother?"

"Like I failed to make you into a race woman."

The elephant was now taking up all the air in the room.

I started hearing Jack Nicholson yelling, *You want the truth, you can't handle the truth.*

"So you think I'm some kind of Oreo?"

I laughed at the term; hadn't heard that one since the seventies. I pulled my little girl to me, hugged her hard and kissed the top of her head.

"No. I don't think that—you're simply a product of your experience and the times. I intellectually understand that, which is why I haven't said anything about his race. There had been progress in the seventies, when I was at Lawrenceville; two of my best friends there were White girls. You didn't know them because Peggy died when you were a little girl and Allison, well, Allison moved to France and we lost touch."

What I didn't tell her was that Allison also decided to become what she was: a privileged White person who bowed out of our friendship when it got too challenging. It was easier for her to envelop herself in Whiteness.

"I really used to think we were on our way to living in a place where color didn't matter so much, but I've lived long enough to see things go backward, to see fear and hate being sold and bought."

"But does it make a difference in your mind that my father was half?"

"Does it to you?"

"No. I never felt anything other than Black."

"I didn't think you did."

"Does love make a difference?"

"Are you in love? And is that enough?"

I wanted to end this conversation more than I wanted a piece of chocolate cake.

"You'd probably be happier if I went with Miles, wouldn't you."

"Now I won't go there. I don't know anything about him, just as you don't. He seems like a nice man but who the hell knows, and I have to tell you, since it's truth-tellin' time, I'm more than a little concerned that at forty-three he's never been married. I might feel better about him if he was divorced, at least he would've tried it."

"So you think there's something wrong with him, just because he's never been married?"

"Yes. I think for a man, with all that he has going, to not have made a commitment to somebody other than himself, there's a problem somewhere. He may be too picky, too selfish, dealing with sexuality issues, any number of things."

"Oh, Ma. Not everybody is psychologically damaged. . . ."

"Yes, we are."

"Ah, you're impossible. Are you ever unsure about anything?"

"Every day, sweetheart, every day."

Aisha finally let it drop, but my groovy, bubbly high had worn off. Picturing Adam and Adam and me and how different I was as a young, idealistic woman had sobered me right up. His being "half" as Aisha said, didn't ever factor into my decision to love him, but I never really felt at peace with my decision not to tell him about the pregnancy, about Aisha. Once I got to Atlanta and away from my life as an Afro-wearing preppy and realized that I was pregnant with Adam's child I tortured myself about what to do—if I told him he would want to do the right thing, because that was the way he was. He'd forgo or postpone his master of the universe dreams, marry me, raise our child, but I would've known all along that he didn't want to be a young father, living a life akin to the one he'd been raised in. I didn't tell him for his sake and for mine. I knew what he wanted and I couldn't be the corporate, country-club wife if my life depended on it. I was too much my daddy's child. Jazz played in my veins. I was a free-styler, an improviser. I couldn't dance the foxtrot even if I'd wanted to.

# Chapter 14

## Burning Down the House

## _Aisha_

When I called Miles it took him weeks to get back to me. Turns out his mother had died and he'd been in Memphis, his hometown. I was surprised at how candid he was with me about his feelings. He said he felt like his insides had just cracked apart: _Now I finally understand what a broken heart feels like. I'd hurt when Alice and I broke up for the final time. The look in Natasha's eyes the night we broke up at our engagement party hurt bad. But that was like heartburn compared to a heart attack—losing my mom, who was my source for everything, my memory, my center, my strength._

He told me how he'd sat with her, holding her hand, talking with her when she'd come in and out of the morphine haze she was under to ease the pain from the cancer that was in her bones. He'd stayed in Memphis for another week, mostly, he said, _just being in her little palace, the piece of heaven I'd bought for her with my first bonus. She was so happy in that house. It was a_

*Palm Beach villa to her. I sat on her plastic-covered living room
sectional, flicking the plasma TV she loved to watch her soaps on;
I'd go from room to room smelling her Giorgio perfume and crying
like the little lost boy I was. I got two haircuts in one week just for
the familial presence of Mr. Banks and the other men who hung
out at Mr. Banks's barbershop. I've never felt so lonely before in my
entire life. Now I was an orphan. Sorry-ass Dad died of diabetes
and liquor and Big Mama had died a decade ago.*

I listened to Miles talk and tried to imagine what it must
feel like to lose your mother. I couldn't. I knew I'd be lost without mine.

"Miles, I'm so sorry. I can't imagine . . ."

"No, I certainly couldn't and I knew she was dying. She
hung on six months longer than the doctors predicted. She
was a tough old bird." He laughed when he said that and then
he abruptly changed the subject.

"I have to admit I am curious about why you, who could
have the world on a string if you marry Will, would be willing
to risk throwing it all away."

"I never thought I didn't have the world on a string," I
laughingly informed him.

He invited me over for a Sunday-night dinner. It seemed
innocent enough although there's nothing innocent about
going to a man's apartment.

When he opened the door, he stood looking as delicious as
Grandma's red velvet cake.

I handed him the bottle of wine I brought and took off my
cream wool coat. I'd decided jeans and a tight short-sleeved
sweater were the right note. Nothing too revealing or that I
wanted him to think I'd spent too much time planning.

"You look great," he said, and kissed me on the cheek.
"Thanks for the wine."

"You're welcome. I didn't know what we were having, so I brought white."

"Ah, it doesn't matter. I made lamb, but then I thought, Maybe she doesn't eat meat like most people in her generation. . . ."

"I'm not like most people in my generation and yes, I eat meat."

"Good."

"Have a seat . . . look around. I just have to sauté the spinach."

I walk into his living room, noticing his varied art collection.

"You collect?"

"What?"

"Art."

"Oh, I wouldn't say that. I see something that I think looks good, I buy it. I couldn't tell you who half the artists are. . . ."

"Somehow I don't believe that," I said, admiring a Philemona Williamson that takes up a good part of a living room wall.

He handed me a glass of red.

"Thanks, mmm, this is good. What is it?"

"It's an inexpensive South African cabernet."

I dribbled a little on my sweater.

"Here, let me get that," he said as he dabbed the spot with a dishtowel.

"I always do that. It's really why I drink white."

"Oh, I can open that one."

"No no, I prefer this. It's wonderful."

His place was very nice, obviously one that most women probably oohed and aahed over. By any standards, especially New York's, it's awesome, but my eye has been widened to see some real, old dough, my standards have been raised.

I walked over to the dining room, the most dramatically decorated room here: chocolate-brown walls with mauve leather insets with hammered brass nails, black wood table and chairs. The table was set with pumpkin- and zebra-colored linens. No doubt a woman had bought these. There was a pretty round glass vase of raspberry-colored Gerber daises in the center.

"Your table is so pretty. Look at this room, this nice china," I said, picking up a white dessert plate that was trimmed in gold polka dots.

"This looks like wedding china. . . . I'm very impressed, Miles. You have great taste."

"Naw. I just bought this one day, I was out and about. My decorator had suggested that I own some nice plates. You like?"

"Love. You sure you're not gay?"

He blushed because he understood this was intended to be a compliment.

"I'm sure."

"A metrosexual then."

"A what?"

"Metrosexual. A straight man who appreciates fine things, who has a good eye, he's in touch with his feminine side."

"Um, I've missed that one. Come on, sit down," he said, pulling a ladder-back chair from the table.

"Is there anything I can help with?"

"Nope, it's all done. Just sit here, have another glass of wine and I'll be right back."

I sat, sipping my cabernet and trying to figure out Miles Browning. Where did he come from and how could he have come so far and still seem so damn unaffected? I knew other Black guys with his level of accomplishment before, but many of them were insufferable, pompous asses. Miles seemed like a down-to-earth, regular guy. There must be more to his story than poor boy from Memphis makes good on Wall Street.

"Voilà," he said as he carried two plates of lamb, sautéed spinach and garlic mashed potatoes into the dining room.

"Comfort food," he announced. "Food to warm you up and put some meat on them bones."

"It looks delicious. Mmm, the smell. And you cooked all this?"

"All what, baby? This ain't nothin'. I been cookin' all my life, practically—I was a latchkey kid and Mama wasn't tryin' to raise no helpless man."

Whenever he talked about his mother or growing up in Memphis his speech and his southern accent became more emphatically Black.

I considered commenting on my observation, but decided not to.

"And the salad is great."

"Okay, so I ordered that from the restaurant."

"Good. I was beginning to get scared."

"Is the salad from Maya?"

"Yes, I noticed how much you liked it."

"Well that was very sweet."

"So, everything okay? I was a little surprised that I hadn't heard from you" he said between bites. "You sounded a little upset on your message."

"Oh, maybe I was when I called, but I'm over that now."

"Anything you want to talk about?"

I blew in exasperation and took another sip, finishing my glass, trying to decide what to reveal.

"Come on now, I'm sure it's not that big a deal."

"No," I said, looking deeply into his eyes for the first time since I got here. "It's not that big a deal."

He poured more wine into my glass. He wanted to know

what was happening between Will and me, but hesitated bringing it up.

"You're probably wondering what the hell I'm doing here?"

"No, I'm . . . I'm well aware that I invited you. You didn't just show up outta the blue. I do have to say that I know you're bothered by something and it is a big deal."

"Yeah, like what the hell am I doing in a strange man's apartment, eating dinner when I have a fiancée and wedding plans and . . ."

"So far, this is all innocent."

"Mmm. I wonder if Will would think so."

"Umm, probably not," Miles said, pouring more wine for himself.

"Well, I think it's wise to have second thoughts, look around, make sure you're sure about the person you're making this huge commitment to . . . nothing wrong with that."

"Why are you pretending that I didn't throw myself at you at the engagement party, for God's sake."

Miles nodded.

"I . . ."

"Yeah, you don't have much to say about that," I said, holding out my glass for another refill.

We finished the bottle.

"Let me get another one. Do you want to open yours? We could have it with dessert."

"Which is?"

"I hope you like sweets—they're my weakness. I got coconut cupcakes with cream cheese icing."

"Ummm. I love sweets too, but I think the white may be a little too much with the cupcakes."

"You're right," he said, lifting my finished plate from in front of me.

"Let me clear the table."

"No, but you can set out the dessert. You want coffee?"

"No, never at night."

"Me either. I'd never get any sleep."

"Me too. I don't know how people do it."

Miles got out a bottle of brandy from a cabinet over the sink and handed it to me along with a tray to put the cupcakes on. Standing next to each other in the galley kitchen was as close as we'd been tonight.

As I lifted a cupcake from the box to put on the tray, a little icing got on my finger. I licked it off with vigor, moaning in the process.

"I told you," he said.

I swiped another finger full of icing, this time turning toward him and putting my sugar-coated finger to his mouth. He licked my finger clean of icing and sucked the length of it into his mouth. I moaned again. And just like that, we went for each other like Jessica Lange and Jack Nicholson in *The Postman Always Rings Twice.*

He grabbed me into him, wrapping his toned arms around me. I pressed my mouth, breasts, torso and pelvis into him. We kissed hard, stopping only to gasp for air between kissing each other's lips, necks, cheeks and chests.

"I've never felt this before," I said, between kisses.

He turned my back to him and lifted my hair to expose my neck, which he licked and kissed until I was asking for him to take me. He caressed my breast with one hand and encircled my waist with the other, pulling me tighter and tighter into him. He felt my nipples stiffen through my cashmere cable knit, inhaling my lime, basil, grapefruit fragrance as if he were becoming intoxicated by it.

I pushed him back, into the Viking stove, rubbing my behind on the bulge in his jeans.

He rubbed both his hands through my hair, massaging my scalp with his thick fingers.

Just when I felt like I was about to let go, he stopped and turned me around. Cupping my face, looking into my eyes asking if I was sure I wanted to do this. I had tears in my eyes and told him that I never wanted anything more. We walked slowly to the bedroom, which was a cocoon of browns and neutrals. The bed sat high in the room and was enveloped in fabric, heavy silk-striped fabric.

We stood against the bed, slowly removing each other's clothes. I unbuttoned his white oxford shirt; he pulled my lavender sweater over my head, exposing a pink nylon bra splashed with red flowers. He looked at my covered breasts, cupped them and kissed my cleavage, inhaling me, rubbing his hands over them, and gently squeezing them. I removed his shirt, exposed a well-defined chest covered in peasy hairs, the top of his boxer underwear peaking out from his jeans. He unhooked my bra and we each shimmied out of our jeans. I wanted to throw off my soggy matching panties, but decided to let him remove them. We stood in front of each other, he cupped my face again, kissing me deeply, filling my face with kisses. I smiled and raised my face to him, exposing my neck, wanting more of his thick hungry tongue. He moved his hands down my face, onto my breasts again, circling the protruding nipples with the tip of his finger and then walking his fingers down my belly into my panties and inside of me.

"I love that you're so wet."

His finger danced around my clit, putting off my imminent peak. He grabbed my behind and hiked me up onto my tiptoes, grinding into me.

"Ohmygod," I yelled out.

He whispered, "May I?"

"I'm begging you to."

He lay back on the bed and I crawled on top of him. Looking deeply into his eyes, I straddled him as he entered me. I inhaled with a sucking sound and we both found our rhythm, rocking only a few moments before I bucked and screamed and hissed, my breasts swinging from side to side, as he fingered my nipples ever so slightly until I let out a sound that let him know I'd arrived. He followed me immediately with less noise but no less intense an explosion.

I stayed in Miles's bed for three days.

# CHAPTER 15
## Mama's Baby, Papa Maybe

## *Camille*

Aisha had demanded to know who her real father was three times during her short life. The first time was when she in pre-school, she must've been four and she wanted to know why her dad didn't live with us. I was dating Lem at the time, but we weren't yet married. Aisha just started calling him Daddy, but couldn't understand why he didn't live with us. Obviously that stopped once we were married and we moved into a house together, but I told her he was her stepfather. She didn't really understand what that meant until middle school, but it wasn't until we divorced when she was twelve that she began to get ugly. The divorce was traumatic for her. She loved Lem and loved our little family life together. She called me all kinds of names when I told her we were leaving and even told me that she wanted to stay with Lem and I could go.

After a while, when we were settled into the two-family

frame house I bought, she came into my bedroom and sat on the edge of the bed one night.

"I want to know who my real father is."

I was propped up in bed, trying to balance the bills and figure out, again, how I was going to pay her tuition that month, cursing under my breath at my loud-ass tenants overhead. I'd reminded them a hundred times that their lease stipulates rugs on the floor. He said he had allergies and couldn't have a rug and at first I'd suggested it nicely, then finally I said, "Well then take off your damn shoes in the house."

"Why won't you let Lem help? Why won't you get my father to help? What's wrong with you?" Aisha yells at me.

She is becoming a teenager now and I realize she is crazy, so I control myself and do not slap her into the next room.

"What's wrong with me? What the hell is wrong with *me*? What's wrong with me is you, you little spoiled ungrateful child. After all I've done for you, keep doing for you, and all you want to know is about some damn fantasy dad? Why do you need to know him? What do you think he can give you that I can't? You're so lucky to have Lem."

Each time the scene ended with me in tears—the only time she witnessed that—and her slamming herself in her room.

The third and final time was when she was in college, after my dad's funeral, I knew she was hurting, but I was in my own deep grief, so intense that my body ached. I was incapable of dealing with her needs but I think I finally recognized the primal need to understand one's origins. I knew I had to tell her about her real father. Daddy had been her first father and when Lem came along she had two. For a while she was satisfied, even seemed happy, and temporarily I was off the hook: she'd stopped asking. But now that Daddy was gone, and Lem was essentially gone too, even though he kept in touch with Aisha, she felt pushed aside.

We'd had the traditional church funeral and later held a big memorial service when Daddy died. All his jazz buddies came out and either spoke or played something. The highlight though was when his favorite singer Carmen McRae sang "Comes Love," "Skylark," which Daddy had recorded with her in 1958, and "His Eye Is on the Sparrow." It was beautiful and just what we needed to bring us back to life again. After the service, we all went back to Mom's house for yet another repast. Seeing Mom and Carmen together, side-by-side, was the first time I realized how much they looked alike. Maybe that was why Daddy liked her so much—although, I think he knew her before he knew Mom. Anyway, the whole room was woozy from too much grief and celebration. The jazz folk who are notorious night folk stayed practically till the sun came up—MJ ended up making omelets and serving mimosas. Mom went to bed, leaving Aisha and I to clean up, which was fine because I hadn't been able to sleep anyway. Aisha, who was now in her third year at UVA, and I were standing at the sink washing and drying Geneva's good crystal glasses when she said something about wanting to find her real dad.

I heard her, but stood frozen, a highball glass in my hand.

She was standing close enough to me so that I could smell the wine on her breath.

"Do you even know who he is or were you just fucking everything in sight?"

Before I realized what had happened, the glass hit the floor and my hand was crossing Aisha's face. I had never touched her in anger before, no spanking, nothing. I didn't believe in that and she was always such a reasonable child, one who I could actually always talk to; but when she said that, I lost it. I hit her so hard that I left my handprint on her face. She stared at me before walking away, her hand tracing the red print on her cheek. She went to a guest room and quietly shut the door. The next day was among the most miserable days I've ever spent as her mother. We avoided each other, she wouldn't respond when I spoke directly to her, only to clarify plans for the following day when I would drive her to the train station. The next day we drove in silence. I felt like I wanted to stop breathing. I'd lost my Daddy and I'd hurt my little girl. That was when I understood, knew I would have to give her something, anything to make up for what I'd done. I'd give her something about her dad. I owed her that.

"I'll walk you inside so we can talk."

Her head down, staring into her lap, she nodded.

I parked the car and we walked into Penn Station. We walked over to a secluded bench in a corner of the station and sat down. I held her hands in mine and looked into her eyes, even though she wouldn't look at me. I began to speak and was surprised at the sound of my own voice. I never thought I'd be here with her, telling her what I was about to tell her.

"I know you have a right to know and it was wrong of me to keep it from you all this time."

She still wouldn't look at me.

"I know you know that I love you with everything inside me. Everything. When I hit you, I hated myself more than you'll know."

She looked at me.

I touched her face gently.

"I've been selfish and foolish and I hope that one day you can forgive me."

Now tears were streaming down her face. I reached into my coat pocket and handed her a piece of a mangled tissue.

"Your father was a boy from Lawrenceville. He was someone I'd loved but at the time, when we graduated, I didn't know I was pregnant. It wasn't until I was at college that I real-ized that I'd been pregnant when I got there."

"So who is he?"

"His name is Adam Sorrell. I haven't seen him since we left Lawrenceville."

"So he was your boyfriend?"

"Yes."

"And did you ever tell him?"

"No."

"Why?"

"I've tried to answer that question so many times; maybe be-cause I was afraid of what he'd say or do."

"Like what?"

"I didn't know at first that you were Adam's, then I thought I wanted to be with Greg, the Morehouse boy, but then he made it clear that I wasn't part of his life plan...."

She looked confused.

"I know it's a lot to process."

"Mom, stop talking to me like a shrink."

I put my arm around her shoulder and tried to pull her toward me. She shifted away, turning her body from me.

"I just don't understand how you could've kept something like this from me, all this time. What were you planning, to never tell me?"

"Sweetheart, I know this sounds lame, but I didn't ever have a plan."

She looked at me and her eyes softened.

"I gotta get my train."

"You need time to think, I know."

She got up and hoisted her backpack onto her shoulder and pulled out the handle to her roller bag.

"You need some help?"

She shook her head and walked away.

"I'll call you later," I said to her back.

I sat back down on the bench and stared at the dust motes dancing in space.

*Do you even know who my father is?*

That question rang in my ears long after Aisha had left for school. How many times had my little girl wondered about it? Was it really over now? It had been so hurtful to see my precious girl in so much pain. What does that do to a child—the not knowing? I couldn't know. I'd known not only parents but grandparents and a collection of my mother's people in Wilmont, Georgia. It was the kind of place where everybody was either actually related by blood or claimed one another as cousin. Back then people raised other people's children so frequently that blood line really was irrelevant. It was about taking care of each other, of looking out, adding an extra cup of water in the soup so that fewer would go to bed hungry, but it was hardly irrelevant to my child.

# CHAPTER 16

# My Dinner with Major

## *Geneva*

I'd never been to a restaurant before. The place had white tablecloths, cheerful curtains, flowers on the table and a pleasant nongreasy aroma, even though the food, fancied-up stuff that I grew up on in Wilmont, was swimming in it.

Everyone greeted Major like the celebrity I later discovered he was. A few of the men came over to the table to shake his hand and reverently left before becoming an intrusion. Major smiled and welcomed all, but made me feel the most special.

"That sure is a pretty dress you're wearing today, Miss Geneva."

I thanked him and begged him to drop the Miss.

"You seem more southern than me."

"We're all from the south, at some point, isn't that right?"

Turns out Major's people hadn't been in the south for two generations. He was from a small town in eastern Pennsylvania, weren't too many Black folk, he said it was Quaker land

and he'd grown up pretty far from the physical and mental scars most southern Blacks suffered.

"Believe me, I had my own, they was just different, that's all," he told me.

"So, how come you don't have a family? A wife?"

"Been married to the music, all these years, I guess. Can't grow somethin' if you ain't standing still."

Our fried-chicken dinners arrived and he ate like he hadn't. I picked at the food, afraid of picking up the chicken with my hands and seeming like the hick I was. What I tasted was better than Mama Sadie's and Mama Sadie could cook.

"I like a girl with an appetite."

I didn't know what to say and felt embarrassed that he knew what I was doing.

"So, when do you go back to Hampton?"

"Tomorrow morning."

"Well, I'd sure like to see you again. Would you mind if I came for a visit?"

"That would be fine, I mean nice."

I didn't know what to say because I didn't know what I'd do with Kenneth.

"We travel down to Washington, D.C. all the time. Hampton's not too far from there. Maybe you could meet me."

"I've never been to Washington, D.C."

"You'd love it. I could get you your own room. Colored folks got hotels and everything there."

"Well, sure. That would be very nice. Can I bring Trudy?"

"Of course; can't have my lady traveling alone."

*My lady*? When did that happen? Oh God, he's moving way too fast, but I did like the sound of it, especially in his hepcat way of talking.

"I know I'm jumping the gun, but that's how I do. I know

what I want and I go out and get it. You, Miss Geneva, are what I want."

"Can I ask you a question?"

"Anything," Major said, shaking hot sauce on his chicken.

"How old are you?"

"I'm thirty years old. Is that too old for you?"

"Well, I don't know. I've never . . ."

"I don't think it is. You're what, twenty? Twenty-one?"

"Twenty-one."

"See, it's perfect. Women mature much faster than men. We're actually about the same age. I'm 'bout ready to settle down now."

"Mmm."

"So, I'm sure you got a dude down there at college. Y'all got a date set yet?"

"A date?"

"You know, the weddin' date?"

"Um, no. We haven't set a date, but we figure, I guess, it'll be sometime the summer after we both graduate."

"Mmmm. And is that what you want to do? I mean, does he make your liver quiver?"

Major laughs so loud the patrons look over, smiling at the joke they missed.

"Well, he's very nice, from a good family. . . ."

"And dry as toast with no jam."

"Major," I scold him, trying to conceal my delight.

"I'm sorry, Miss—I mean Geneva. I don't mean to offend."

"I'm not offended."

"So, you gonna come meet me in Washington, D.C.?"

"I'll have to see."

"Fair enough. I'll call you close to the time and if your schedule allows it, there'll be a ticket waiting for you and Trudy at the train station."

I knew as surely as I was sitting there that I would meet that man in Washington, D.C. I'd a met him on the moon if he'd asked.

Needless to say, I returned Kenneth's pin as soon as I got back to school. He didn't seem too upset, just looked at the pin in his palm, tossed it up once and then put it into his shirt pocket. I felt like I'd just been one of any number of girls who could've become Mrs. Kenneth Johnson C. Smith.

Obviously, Major and I got together.

Trudy and I went to Washington, D.C. where he was performing for two nights. We had a room at the Brown's Inn, a lovely old house that would now be called a bed-and-breakfast. We got married later that year, after I'd graduated, in Wilmont and before anything was showing. Mama Sadie made my dress of satin and tiny beads around the sweetheart neck and the hem, but never commented on my bulging middle or Major's profession, but I felt embarrassed and promised myself and God that day that we would live a Christian life and make Mama Sadie proud. Our wedding and reception was held at the church and everyone in town was invited. Some of Major's jazz friends played and while the people of Wilmont had never heard jazz, they'd thought of it as "the devil's music." He won a few converts that day, because everybody had a good time and even said it wasn't the kind of music they'd expected. It was nice and soothin' almost like a hymn.

I tried to give my children something upstanding, that's all I was trying to give Camille and Major Junior. My son didn't seem to have any problem at all with what I was trying to teach, but Miss Missy, well she was always the rabble-rouser, always questioning, always causing problems. Couldn't just take me at my word that everything I was doing I was doing for their betterment: No, she got to be callin' me a phony and tellin' me I was always "tryin' to act White." Wasn't nobody tryin' to be like them. I could care less frankly and both Major and I was happy when we didn't have to deal with 'em at all. Camille just didn't see that. I was just trying to give them a chance so they wouldn't get caught doing some old job they hated, something with no dignity like so many of our people had to do. Mama Sadie, her mother, grandmother, great-grandmother, legions of Black women raising White folks' children while their own oftentimes got the short end of the stick, practically having to raise themselves 'cause their own Mama was all mothered out, had spent it all on the White children. White children who didn't even have to give them the respect to not call them by their first names; those White children who Black women fed, taught, loved many times loved them back, but weren't taught that they should respect them. But those women did what they had to do to put food on the table. I wanted my kids to be respected in life and I knew you couldn't get that havin' babies without a husband or an education. I wanted them to live on a higher level, be treated like full human beings. Is there anything wrong with that? Camille wanted to fight me all the way. She was a rebel, I guess she got it honest, she was like Major. I know Aisha's giving it to her now, though, marrying a White boy and all. Yeah, Camille, Miss Black America, is getting a feel for what it's like when the person you love most and who you've done the most for, turns around and spits on all your dreams for them.

# CHAPTER 17

# MIA with Blig

*Aisha*

I didn't leave Miles's apartment for three days. We didn't. We ordered food in, made love and talked. He was grieving and I was the distraction he needed. I couldn't remember ever feeling truly needed.

"My mother was everything to me," he said as we ate breakfast in bed. I understood that he didn't mean this as an understatement.

"She was my center," he said, looking at me as if to say, *Do you have any idea what that's like?*

"Do you think you were so close because it was just the two of you?"

He sipped his coffee and held his mug in his hand, rubbing one side of it absentmindedly.

"Oh, no question. If my dad had been around, I woulda spent time with him too, but it was just me and Earlene. . . ."

"What was she like?"

He looked at me gratefully, put down his mug and inhaled deeply.

"She was funny. She liked to cook, she was wise, she was strong and she really knew me and understood early on what I was going to need."

"What do you mean?"

"Well, we were poor, we were on welfare more often than not, but she didn't raise me to think of myself as poor or deprived. We just didn't have money, but she would read the paper, read adult stuff out loud to me, she was constantly finding free programs and stuff at the libraries and museums. Foundation-sponsored stuff like camp and schools. That's how I got to Harvard. She found some program that paid for me to go to prep school. My mother wasn't afraid, that's the biggest thing I got from her."

"She sounds amazing."

His sadness was palpable. "She was.

"The first thing I did when I started making money was buy her a house. We always lived in little rundown rented houses. She used to do dayswork—you don't even know what that is, do you?"

"I do. It's domestic work, like a maid."

"Yeah, so she'd do dayswork out in Whitehaven, which is a kinda ritzy section of Memphis. Well, that's where I bought her house. It was just a four-bedroom house, but to her it was a Palm Beach villa. She was so happy there."

"So, you were there with her when she passed away?"

"Yup, I was holding her hand. I held her hand for two weeks as she slipped away from me. I can still smell her perfume."

"Did you have a relationship with your dad before he died?"

As soft and open as he was about his mother, he was as closed and hard about him.

"We didn't have a relationship. He skipped out on my mom when I was barely able to walk."

"Do you know what happened, I mean between them?"

"Naw, not really. All I could piece together was he wanted to go chasing the dream of a better life up north and she didn't want to go. He moved to Detroit, worked in one of the car factories and basically drank himself to death. He had diabetes and high blood pressure. He lost a leg and his eyesight before he died, but he never gave up drinking."

"That's so sad. I don't know what makes people do things like that. Did you ever make peace with your father?"

"If by peace you mean forgive him, no I didn't ever forgive him for leaving us but I did make peace with him as a person, separate from him as my father."

"What do you mean?"

"I mean, he was just a man, a Black man trying to survive in a place that wasn't interested in seeing you succeed. Who knows what he went through living in the south in those days. A lot of Black folk just left without knowing what they were going to, just that anything had to be better than what they lived in the South, with no opportunity, no nothing."

"He must've been so proud of you? Did he ever remarry or have any other kids?"

"No, he didn't and yeah, I guess he was proud."

Miles clenched his jaw and I knew this was probably the end of this topic.

"I never talked to people about this. I don't know why I'm doing it with you."

He got up from the table and went into his library and closed the door.

We could both use a little time alone.

I had been MIA for three days. I called in sick to the job I hated. Miles was helping me construct the job that I really did want and was helping me figure out how to go after it. The only person who knew where I was was Cedra, who was barely speaking to me.

"Ash, this is so ridiculous," she'd said when I called her.

"I know I know."

"Have you left the bed in three days?"

"To eat and go to the bathroom. We've had a few meals in the dining room."

"So, what are you going to tell Will?"

"I don't know."

"This is just some stupid acting-out bullshit, you do know that?"

"Mmm-hmm."

"And you don't care?"

"Not right now I don't."

"So he's got some kind of mojo over you?"

"You could probably say that."

"What is he like, the Black Big—Blig?"

I laughed out loud at that one.

"Blig. Yeah, he's definitely the Black Mr. Big, that's him."

I couldn't begin to explain myself to Cedra, since I didn't understand what I was doing myself, all I did know was I felt like metal to his great big horseshoe magnet.

Miles and I talked, really talked. We'd both been raised by amazing single mothers and had biological fathers who were totally absent from our lives. He knew who his father was but had only seen him a few times in his life and he understood deeply what it was like to not know the other part of yourself.

"You should go and find him," he told me.

"For what?"

"For you. It'll help you."

"I'm fine with it."

"You are? And that's why you fucking up left and right, 'cause you're fine."

"What're you talking about?"

We were having grits and fish in bed. I hadn't combed my hair or brushed my teeth.

"You hate your job. You're engaged but you're here with me. You spend more money than you make. Do I have to go on?"

"Well, I didn't know you were such a critic."

"I ain't criticizin', baby, I just see, that's all. We all gotta deal with our shit in some way and this is how you're dealing—"

"What shit?"

"Ish, come on, baby. This is Miles. I been there. It's alright. You ain't gotta front with me."

I put my tray on the nightstand.

He put his fork down and looked at me welling up.

He pushed his tray away and pulled me into his arms.

"It's okay, baby," he said, holding me and cradling my head. "Go on, let it all out."

I couldn't speak as I cried for things I'd long put away. I cried for all that I'd carried, I cried for my mother, for my father, for what I was doing to Will; for what I had done to myself.

I just hadn't even realized that I wasn't just fine.

"What have I done?"

"Nothin' that can't be fixed. You need to start with findin' your daddy."

I didn't want to leave Miles's apartment, this cocoon of safety. I couldn't figure out how I could feel so at home with someone I hardly knew, but I did. I'd never let even Will see me without my hair or face done. With Miles I hadn't even washed my face. I wore one of his T-shirts and an old cashmere cardigan the entire time I was there and felt prettier than I ever had in my life. When I started to get light-headed from being inside for two days, we went onto his terrace and I wore his Ugg slippers and his overcoat over his sweatpants and the cardigan. I wore the same thing when I finally went back home.

When Will asked me where I'd been, I lied that I'd been at Cedra's. He just let it go. He'd left several unanswered messages on my cell, and when I told him I just needed to be left alone he said he understood. Maybe this is what my mother means when she says they're different—the very rich. I told him that I'd needed space and just went to Cedra's for a couple days and he just bought it. Didn't ask any questions, why didn't you call, why didn't you answer your cell phone, none of that, just okay, hope you're feeling better about things. Maybe he'd done his own dirt, something fucked up that he's not telling me. The following weekend we drove out to his grandmother's place in Long Island.

We entered Will's grandmother's house at night through the back door, so it wasn't until the blinding sun came over the water the next morning that I saw the extent of this "cottage." There must have been an acre in front that meandered to the ocean. The place was decorated in aqua and pale green in nearly in every room; the antique Elvan was so fine, I didn't want to walk on it even barefoot. Will plopped down on one of the down-filled chintz-covered sofas in his dirty jeans and I thought, My mother would kill you for doing that. I didn't say anything, though, because I understood that he'd done this all his life. The grandmother was away in Newport at her other "cottage," the palace that we were planning to hold the wedding. The rug I recognized as the real version of so many fakes in homes of my nouveau riche high school pals that I'd spent so much time in when I was growing up. The very girls I'd felt I had to lie to in order to fit in. One time when I was at Newark Academy after Mom had left Daddy, I pretended I still lived there and had the mother of my friend drop me off there. I still had gate privileges as the stepchild, so the guard waved us in. When we got to the house, of course no one was home. Daddy was at work, but I told the mother it was fine to just leave me there. I was twelve and old enough to be home alone—a lie, but she bought it and left. I had to walk the three-quarters of a mile in the rain to the gatehouse, where the guard took pity on me and loaned me an umbrella. I walked four miles to my real home in the hood. It was pathetic, but I couldn't bear for them to see the crooked little rundown house my mother had moved us to.

This, Will's grandmother's house, is what the strivers were all trying to emulate.

I joined Will outside where he was already doing laps in the swimming pool.

"Good morning," he yelled to me. It was past noon and I'm wrapped in a blanket, having a bad cup of coffee.

"Come in, join me," he yelled, before going back under.

I sat there, feeling so off-kilter after just having been with Miles—why the hell had I agreed to come here? Plus, it was barely April.

Will continued to yell for me to come in and I waved him off, pretending I was just enjoying sitting there, when in fact I was wondering what to do with my hair once it gets wet, mentally scanning the beauty products I'd packed and wondering if I had a scarf.

"It's too cold."

"It's heated. My grandmother keeps it like bathwater."

"Let me finish this and I'll come in. . . ."

I was wearing a T-shirt and black boyfriend panties when I took off my blanket and guest-issue waffle weave robe; Will pretended to lustfully lick his lips.

I eased in, throwing away my twenty-five-dollar Dominican blow dry, happy to find the warm water must be eighty degrees and swam to him. We swapped spit, as he liked to call it.

"You have the most perfect breasts," he said, pushing them together through my now wet T-shirt.

"You'd better stop before you start something. . . ."

"That's just what I was hoping."

After our quickie against a pool wall we swam and floated till we got hungry.

There were salads of various kinds made by his grand-mother's help and covered in the refrigerator. I got out of the pool and wrapped myself up in my robe and blanket, trying to warm up as I waited for Will to bring out the food. He'd dressed in corduroy pants and a ratty old Williams College sweatshirt and brought out an array of chicken and tuna salad, green salad and two loaves of cibatta.

I didn't move because I was so cold.

"I've never seen your hair like that," Will said, setting down the food on the table.

"Like what?"

"Like that, wild and curly . . ."

"Wild and curly?" I repeated, with an attitude.

"I like it. Why don't you ever wear it like that?"

He was now chomping down, talking with his mouth half full of food.

"It's really sexy."

I hate the way I sometimes feel around him, like some juicy, dusty specimen. I've tried to tell him this, but he doesn't get it. "I'm more than my hair, my breasts and my looks."

He says, "Why can't you just take the compliment. I find you incredibly attractive. What's wrong with that?"

I let it drop.

He got up from where he sat across from me at the wrought iron patio table and lifted my face between his hands and kissed me.

"You are so gorgeous. I want to eat you."

He knelt before me, pushing the blanket away, boyfriend panties and my legs apart, placing his face between my thighs.

# CHAPTER 18

# Hardest Thing to Do
# Is to Bury a Child

## *Camille*

Word came of Adam's death through my alumni bulletin. I couldn't imagine it was by natural causes. I assumed he died of a broken heart, a broken man who'd not been able to fully leave his past behind. Who can?

The obituary said he'd been working for legal services in Buffalo. Not a way to get rich, build a fortune. He did, as he'd said he would—went to business school and did a combined law degree. It read that he'd worked on Wall Street before joining the ranks of the noble poor, just as his mother would've wanted. I called MJ, the only person I knew who knew people we'd gone to school with, to get the inside dope, the stuff that would never be in an obituary. MJ said it had been a drug overdose; that Adam had been using heroin for years. He'd tried to clean up, went to rehab several times, but heroin was

one of those passions that wouldn't be left behind. He had an
ex-wife, a Muffy he'd met at Dartmouth and married after
graduate school at Harvard; they hadn't had children; apparently she wanted to wait until he progressed beyond associate
level at the Wall Street firm. When he left to heed the call to
work for the poor, she booked. I imagined Adam, filling his
veins to numb himself from feeling all that he was capable of,
and I felt so sad right now for what might've been. What if I'd
told him? How would his life have been different? Our lives?
What would Aisha's life have been like?

The obit said he was survived by his mother, an Abby Sorrell of Washington, D.C.

I didn't spend any time thinking about it. I got on the
phone, called Lawrenceville and got Adam's mother's number.
I called her in D.C., told her I'd been his friend and that I
wanted to come and see her.

She sounded friendly, if a little spacey, on the phone, but
told me her address and said she worked at a food co-op where
her hours varied, but just either call the store or her home
when I arrived and we'd get together.

I went on the next Saturday. Took the train down, called
her from Adams Morgan, the neighborhood where she lived
and worked, and she gave me directions to her apartment.

She lived over a Moroccan restaurant. The hallway up to
her place was painted a dark avocado with gold on the mold-
ings and smelled of eggplant and garlic. She stood at the top of
the stairs after she'd buzzed me in.

"Hey, is that Camille?"

I looked up at her, not able to get more than that she was
thin and looked too young to be Adam's mother.

"It's me," I said, as I huffed after walking a few steps.

"Come on up. I've made us some lunch."

I gathered my skirt and trudged some more up the wooden stairs, grateful for my comfortable clogs.

We stood at the small landing and she stretched out her arms to put a hand on each of my shoulders. She appraised me.

"It's nice to meet one of Adam's friends," she said warmly.

"Thank you." I didn't know what else to say. "It's nice to meet you too."

"Come on in, excuse the mess. I've got cats, hope you're not allergic."

"Oh, me too, not to worry."

On closer inspection, her face was deeply lined and her long, once-blonde hair was more gray than blonde now. She looked pretty much as I'd expected an aged hippie to look— jeans, a gauzy tunic top, scratchy-looking wool socks under Birkenstocks. There were pictures of Adam on the tables, near her altar that featured a Buddha, a little gong made of brass, a photo of Adam and another man, candles and some dried flowers. She also had many childhood drawings up, in home-made frames.

"Is this where he lived with you?"

She looked around the crammed living room with its futon couch, beaded curtains, Tibetan rugs, stacks of books and magazines, and said no.

"We lived in this neighborhood though, but in a bigger apartment, where he had his own room. I used to love it here, before all this gentrification. Adam never did."

I looked down at all the balls of fur and tried to picture the fastidious Adam I knew living like this.

"So, you and Adam must have been good friends?"

"Yeah, we were, but we lost touch after Lawrenceville."

"Were you, like a thing? A couple?"

She was nodding at me, her green eyes dancing.

"Um, yeah. We became that. We started out as just friends and then . . ."

"Those are the best relationships. I'm glad to see you're Black."

Her frank flakiness threw me off. She was an unusual combination. I didn't know what to say, but I knew that this was a person who said whatever bounced to the front of her mind.

"I know that didn't come out right, but I mean we tried to teach Adam to be open, that we're all connected, that the barriers between us are false, put there by the ruling structure to keep us distracted from the real problem, all in a kind of prison."

The kettle blew and she seemed startled.

"Saved from my down-with-the-man speech," she said, chuckling at herself.

She got up.

"What kind of tea can I get you? I have a really good Moroccan; it'll keep you up for days."

"Sounds good. I'll have that one."

She went into the kitchen and I sat in a flower-print arm chair.

"Can I help?" I yelled to her after a minute.

"Nope, everything's already set up."

I looked at her coffee table, which was covered with periodicals: *Smithsonian; Mother Jones; Vegetarian Life; Yoga Journal; The Village Voice* and a few free D.C. weeklies.

She came back with a tray with two mugs of tea and an assortment of hard-looking biscuits with raisins, a small bowl of hummus, one of dates and figs, and some salad greens.

"I hope this isn't too crunchy for you. Oh, I forgot the peanut butter," she said, jumping up to go back to the kitchen.

"It looks good," I lied, thinking, I need to eat more like this and less stuff fried in grease.

"So," she said, setting down the organic peanut butter on the tray, which was precariously perched on top on the coffee table/library.

"These biscuits were just made today. Try some, I know they don't look it, but they're delicious. Whole wheat flour, safflower, maple syrup, no yeast . . ."

I took one from the basket and bit. She was right.

"Told ya. We can't keep 'em in at the co-op. People come all the way from Capitol Hill to buy them, especially now with all this low-carb crap."

"Why do you call it crap?"

"'Cause it is. Our bodies need carbs. It's just foolishness for people to cut out fruit. Americans are so gullible, but enough about that. You didn't come all this way to hear me rant."

I watched Abby and smiled at her fondly.

"Well, I have to tell you that I didn't do much thinking about why I was coming here. I read Adam's obit and just felt so bad and weirdly at a loss. I felt like I had to do something."

"You know how he died?"

I nodded that I did.

"He was such a little straight-ass when he was kid. Hated people hanging around our apartment smoking dope; hated that we didn't live in a nice little suburban house, that his dad didn't look like everybody else's dad."

"Yeah, he told me about it."

"He did? What'd he tell you?"

I didn't want to go into what he'd said. I was afraid to hurt her feelings or tell her something he never wanted her to know.

"We were very close, once," she said, as if reading my mind. "He used to tell me everything, but when his dad died, he just became so angry and so withdrawn. I couldn't reach him anymore."

"I guess that's when I met him."

"Was he happy at Lawrenceville?"

"At the time I would've said yes, but in retrospect, who knows. We survived it, feeling, being outsiders, we kind of banded together in our weirdness."

"Were you in love?"

I thought about her question, realizing I'd never been asked it before, never talked about Adam like this with anyone. I thought about his rueful, one-dimple smile, his subversive sense of humor, his hazel-green eyes, shaped exactly like hers.

"Yes, we were in love and you have a granddaughter."

"What?"

I knew this wasn't the right way to tell her, but I couldn't think of a right way and also knew that Abby could roll with it.

She tilted her head the way dogs do when they hear something humans can't.

"I never told Adam. He didn't know. We were already at our different colleges and I was seeing someone else . . ."

"You have to give me a minute, Camille," she said, putting her hand on her chest, as if to slow her heart to process the news.

"I know, I'm sorry, I shouldn't have just sprung it like that."

"No, no, it's okay. I just need a minute. You've given me a gift. I need time to appreciate it."

I sat waiting for her to give me a cue that I could go on.

She smiled at me as if I'd just physically presented her with a grandchild, a baby wrapped in a soft pink blanket.

"Go on, tell me everything. Why you decided not to tell him?"

"I was pulling away from Adam. We were far apart, I figured . . . and at first I didn't realize that the baby was his."

"You must've been a baby yourself. How old were you?" she said sweetly.

"Eighteen, nineteen when she was born."

"So, what happened? Did you get married? Does she know? What's her name?"

I smiled at this kind soul in front of me: the best of Adam.

"Her name is Aisha and I raised her for a while alone, um, and I got married when she was seven and divorced when she was about twelve. But she has a really nice stepfather."

She put her fingers to her chin, seemingly to stop it from trembling

"My God. When can I meet her? Does she know about Adam?"

"She knows now and I'm sure she'd love to meet you."

I stayed with Abby for the rest of the day, talking well into the night, running on more than the Moroccan tea.

"So what's she like? What does she do? Where does she live? You know I have no other children. No grandchildren, well, until now."

"Yes, I know that Adam was an only child. This time must be awful for you."

"You know, Camille, it's strange. For a long time Adam has been gone from me, pretty much since he left for boarding school."

"Which he said you didn't want for him."

"Ah, he said that? That's not quite true. His grandmother and I agreed it would be worth a try to send him away. We'd tried other things, after his father died, and nothing worked. It was school or the juvenile-delinquent house the way he was going."

"Really? He never told me that."

"I know. He needed to blame me for everything, even his dad's death, he blamed me."

"Why? If I'm not being too . . ."

"Oh, no we're practically family now, Camille. No, his dad had cancer and before we went the traditional medical route, he was being treated within our community with more-alternative medicines, herbs and such. Adam kept telling us to just take him to the hospital, which his dad didn't want, but Adam thought if I had made him, forced the issue, his dad would have gone and would've been miraculously cured. It was very sad to watch my little boy watch his dad die."

"He never told me all this."

"Did you know his dad was Black?"

"Yeah, I knew that, but a lot of other people at Lawrenceville didn't."

She shook her head at that news.

"You're telling me he was passing?"

"No, no, I don't think so. He just didn't see the need to go around telling people. He was kind of ambiguous about race. . . ."

"So what did he tell you?"

"He didn't have to tell me anything about that. I could look at him and tell; Black people usually recognize other Black people."

I thought about the things he did share with me, and felt right now she needed to have anything I did know, especially now that her son was gone from her forever.

"What he told me was that his dad died and that was when he applied to Lawrenceville, on his own."

"Ha! He didn't know a Lawrenceville from Lawrence Welk!"

I didn't say anything, just looked at her with a weak smile.

"You know, later, after his Wall Street phase, we were talking a lot again. He would call me regularly when he was in Buffalo, like once a week. We'd talk about his cases. It was so much work at legal services. I was proud of what he was doing, helping poor people. I felt like we were going to be close again."

She began to cry.

"But then, I guess the drugs . . . Excuse me," she said.

I suddenly became aware that my body was stiff from sitting in the chair for hours. I got up to stretch and to use the bathroom.

When we resumed in the living room she'd gathered her composure.

"I guess I hadn't realized how much . . ."

"Of course, they say it's the most painful thing to bury a child."

"I have my faith, it's kept me together."

"Yes," I said, looking over at her shrine to Buddha, "I can see that."

"So, tell me more about my granddaughter."

"Well, she's twenty-six. She's beautiful and smart and she's engaged."

"Oh my. What's he like?"

"Well, he's a nice boy. He's her age, they met at work, they're in advertising in New York. He's White," I said, nodding in her direction, as if to say, *You'd approve.*

"What's his background like?" she asked, suspiciously, as if to say, *What kind of White?*

"Well, he's from a very wealthy background."

"Ah, Aisha moves into the upper reaches. That's wonderful," she said, clapping her hands together conspiratorially.

"Yes, well, I haven't made peace with it. . . ."

"Camille, dear, it's her life. Just be there for her, if I can give you unsolicited advice."

I exhaled and relaxed into the surprisingly comfortable chair.

"Yeah, you're right, but you know I'm a mother."

"I know and it's something we always are, no matter what."

I left her at midnight for my little hotel not far away. I would be leaving the next day.

We hugged each other hard and long at the door and I promised that I'd be back soon, with Aisha next time.

# CHAPTER 19

# Not into Fish

## Aisha

"I felt like a total slut."

"I can't imagine why."

"Come on, Cedra, give me a break. You gonna eat your popover?"

"Damn, girl, here. Where does it go?"

I smiled at her as I spread strawberry butter on her popover, my second.

"All that screwing, I guess," Cedra said, holding up her coffee cup for the waitress to bring a refill.

I decided to ignore her. She'd been studying hard at night, working long hours during the day. I'd give her a pass for being so damn nasty.

"You drink too much coffee."

"I know, but how else do you think I get everything done."

"Well, I'm glad you decided to fit me into your schedule. I know how busy you are."

"I figured you need some adult supervision."

I finished eating my popover and momentarily was happily preoccupied by my full stomach.

"So, what the hell are you going to do?"

"I haven't a clue. Maybe nothing, maybe I'll just have them both. Men do it all the time."

"Mmm, but you're not a man and even if you could do it, how long do you think that would last?"

"I don't know. Till I get caught."

Cedra was not sharing my lightheartedness.

"Aisha, you gotta manage this thing. You're running out of time. What're you gonna do, cheat on Will after you're married?"

Now I knew we were entering dangerous territory. Because of what her dad did to her mother, Cedra is vehemently opposed to people who cheat in marriage.

"I wouldn't do that, Cedra."

"I would hope not, but the way you've been acting lately—"

I needed to quickly change the subject or one of us was going to get hurt.

"So, I told you that my job got downsized?"

"No, you didn't. When did that happen?"

"Last week. I'm fine, though, I got a nice severance and it's giving me a chance to think about what I really want to do."

"I know this is a stupid question, but have you started looking for another job?"

"Cedra, I just said I'm trying to figure out what I really what to do. Maybe I'll become a fashion designer, go to FIT. I wanted to do that, remember?"

"I remember, and then you realized you'd have to learn how to sew and you decided that wasn't your thing."

"Yeah, it was hard, but maybe I'm ready to try it again. I'll think of something. Will thinks it's a good idea to take some time off."

"And what, he's going to subsidize you?"

"What is up with you? Why are you being so damn hostile? I'm sitting here trying to understand that you're under a lot of stress, but you are just being too much, you're being such a bitch."

I couldn't take it anymore. I was breathing hard and my adrenaline was pumping. Cedra looked pissed and I didn't know what to expect. We'd never really had a huge fight before, only little bickering sessions over the years that we always let cool by putting time and space between us, never discussing the blowup, just moving on. This, however, would not be one of those times. We were at a place in our lives where we had to deal with our stuff. Either we were going to have it out and not be friends or be better for it. But we had to have it out.

Cedra sat there sipping her coffee, obviously angry.

"All I was trying to say is I don't think you need to be leaning on him now, especially when you're fucking somebody else."

"And you seem to have a real problem with what I'm doing?"

"Yeah, I do. I think it's fucked up. You need to just be up front about it, not all this underhanded shit."

"And is this about me, Cedra, or is this your shit?"

"What're you trying to say, Ash? If you have something to say, you need to just say it."

"Well, I think you have this holier-than-thou thing because of what your father did to your mother and since you haven't dealt with your issues—"

"Whoa, whoa, Miss Thing, you are the last person to be talking about somebody not dealing with their issues. I may—"

"Oh, I'm not saying I don't have mine, but I do talk about them and try to deal with them; you just roll them up and carry them under your arm, like another damn blueprint."

I'd hit her hard, but I had to and we both knew it.

"Well, I'm so sorry that I'm not interested in the lastest handbag and all that other deep stuff that occupies you."

"Oh, so it's like that. You're going to start insulting my dreams because I hit a nerve. Look, Cedra, I know I'm far from perfect, but I also know that you are afraid to feel anything, so scared you might get hurt again and that's no way to live."

The waitress came over to leave the check.

"You've been on me for a while now and I've been trying to overlook it, knowing that you're working so hard, but even with that a real friend would be able to give me some love."

Cedra glared at me.

"Look, you have no idea what I'm up against. Women get their asses kicked in my profession and a Black woman, oh forget it. Look, I gotta go."

She grabbed her wallet and threw her credit card on the table.

"I have money. You don't have to pay for me."

"No, it's alright. I got it."

We sat there in silence waiting for the waitresses to take the card.

It seemed like forever. I was never good at the silent thing. Finally with the check paid we walked out onto the street, already filled with people: young families out with strollers and babies attached; runners; groups of girlfriends having brunch; boyfriends doing the same.

"So, I guess you're going home to work?"

"Yeah," she said, not looking at me. "I have a work thing to go to tonight."

"You going alone?"

Now she looked at me.

"Aisha, of course, don't I always. I'm not seeing anyone—"

I see a tall, fudge-colored, bald, Etro-dressed brother.

"Look, look, he's cute."

Cedra turns, looks over her shoulder and turns back.

"Gay."

"How do you know? You looked at him for a second?"

"Way too well groomed, okay?"

I looked after the cute guy who'd now passed us. His sunglasses, fitted camel blazer, jeans and thick-soled suede shoes were all just so.

"Trust me. Did you notice how he didn't even look at us?"

"I did notice that."

"Hello? Between the two of us, we're somebody's type. You with the long, straight hair, thin and fashionable; me, the butch hair, hip glasses, we've got both extremes covered. He didn't even pretend to notice us. I could just hear him saying to himself, *Not into fish,* as he sashayed by."

I burst out laughing. "You are too damn funny."

Cedra smiled, I think her first today. "You know I'm right."

We get to the intersection of Seventy-second Street and Amsterdam.

"I'm not ready to leave you. Don't you think we should talk some more?"

"Look, darlin', I gotta get some sketches done before this thing tonight."

"Is it something special?"

"Kinda."

"What're you gonna wear?"

"Ash, you know the answer—either my cream suit or the black one."

"Can you at least wear a bright shirt or is that against the architects' union code? You can borrow my new Pucci blouse."

"Pucci? And how're you buying Pucci? You have no job."

"I bought it before I quit, got downsized, whatever. It would look great on you."

"No thanks, sweetie. Listen, try to stay out of trouble. I'll call you tomorrow."

With that Cedra kissed me on the cheek and dashed across Amsterdam. As soon as she was out of eyesight I felt dread.

What was I doing? I was sad about our conversation and what it meant for where we were headed. Were we growing apart as childhood friends often seem to. She may not be interested in examining her life. She may be perfectly content with having only her work. Who am I to say there's something wrong with that. Perhaps she's just angry that I'm sitting on two great guys and she can't get a date.

The weather was just starting to show signs of spring. It was still in the forties but upper and today was one of those rare bright California-like sunny days in New York. I decided to walk through the park and pop in on Will. He lived in one of those rarefied buildings on Fifth Avenue with two addresses, where the old guard uses the more discreet side street address for correspondence, rather than the more obvious, I-got-money, I-live-on-Fifth-Avenue one. And when I got there it all became clear why he was so "oh take all the time you need" when I did my little disappearing act with Miles. I get to his apartment and he's with Amanda, an old childhood friend, who was just leaving, was just saying good-bye.

Now did he really think I was stupid or just so much in love that I'd overlook the fact that it was obvious that Amanda hadn't just popped by but had been there for a while—maybe spent the night?

"Oh hey, babe," he says, all casual as he opens the door.

There's Amanda, thin, blond and perfectly dressed in a thin shearling jacket, tucking her Marc Jacobs purse under her arm.

"Hey, Amanda, this is Aisha."

"Oh, Aisha, it's so nice to finally meet you. I've heard all about you."

She said it in that perfectly bitchy nice way that all these girls seem to learn how to do at Dalton in pre-K.

I hated her on sight and it was obvious to me that she felt the same.

"Thanks, nice to meet you too."

"Can't wait for the wedding, are you all ready?"

"Pretty much, just a few last-minute things to tend to."

"I'm sure it's going to be special."

*Special:* another one of those nice-sounding words that coming from this person means, *I'm sure it's going to be all wrong.*

"Well, yes."

"Okay, well I'll leave you two. I'm sure you want to be alone."

What a bitch.

I'm thinking I can practically smell the sex under her fruit-scented hair. Will is acting all affectionate and fidgety after she leaves.

"So, this is a surprise. I thought you were with Cedra."

"I was. She had to work, as usual."

"Well," he came toward me, kissing me on the cheek, "it's nice to see you."

"Will, cut the shit. What is going on?"

"What're you talking about?"

I give him a nigga-please look.

"What were you and Amanda doing before I came?"

"Oh, she was just leaving."

"That, I saw. Before she was leaving?"

"Oh, we'd had a cup of coffee. She just got back in town. She's been living in London. Our families are old friends, her grandmother lives in the building—"

"And she just felt like fucking?"

"Oh, Ish, come on."

His protests were so fake I couldn't stand to look at him.

"Will, you come on. I could tell I walked in on something. Don't do this. Just admit it. We're not married yet, you're technically still free."

"So, what are you saying—you don't care?"

"Well, I'm saying just admit it, I'm not going to make a big deal out of it. I believe you, you've known her all your life. I know how those relationships are."

He looked at me skeptically like he wasn't sure he could trust what I was saying.

"Look, she's just a friend."

"Does she belong to the heirs' club? What does her daddy own?"

I heard myself spit this out and didn't like how I sounded or felt. I was the one people looked at and said, *Who died and made her Grace Kelly?* or *Who does she think she is?* I never looked at others that way, but I was doing it know.

"Ish, what's the matter with you?"

"Nothing's the matter. Look, I gotta go."

I turned to walk out and he grabbed my arm with more force than I'd ever seen him exert.

"Wait. You can't just walk in here, accuse me of fucking around and just leave."

I look at him like, *You better let go of my arm before I show you the nigga bitch I can be.*

"Come here," he said, pulling me into his chest.

"I don't want anybody else but you. You know that."

I felt fake in his arms.

I stood there, with my arms by my sides, waiting for him to let go.

We stood facing each other in the doorway, me standing in the hall of the building, he in the apartment foyer.

"I really do have to go. I shouldn't have come. I'll talk to you later. . . ."

This time he doesn't try to stop me, just stands there and nods, looking dejected.

"I'll call you later," I heard him say as the elevator doors closed.

# CHAPTER 20

# I Used to Love Him

## *Geneva*

I don't ever think of myself as an old woman. It's not that I'm going around in denims with half my tail hanging out or that I bleach my gray hair blond. I dress and carry myself as a seventy-two-year-old woman should, but I eat right, keep my weight under control and walk around the block a few times a week. How I ended up falling, knocking myself practically unconscious and losing teeth, I don't know. All I know was when I woke up I was on my bathroom floor and there was some blood and teeth down there with me. I got myself up to the phone and reluctantly called Camille. I was reluctant because I knew she'd come in here and just start telling me the house was too much and I needed to think about selling it and moving into *one of those nice retirement homes.*

And I'll have to tell her for the fortieth time that I am not moving into a home. I don't care how nice it is. I'd just as soon die first. Anyway, here she comes, her tail waddling down the hall, calling for me as if I might've gone to the disco or somethin'.

"Just come on in here and help me get to the bed."

I hear her running now, which she should've been doing all along.

I heard her gasp.

"What took you so long?"

"Oh, Mom, what happened?" she said, squatting down to pull me up from under my arms.

"Can you walk? Can you stand up?"

I put one foot down steady but had to lean on her to get to the bedroom.

"I'm alright. I don't think anything's broken."

We limped together till she got me to the bench at the foot of my bed.

"Let me get a washcloth and clean off your face."

I could feel that liquid had dried on my cheek.

She put the warm cloth on my face and held it there.

"I can do it," I said, pushing her hand away, nastier than I should have.

"I'm calling the doctor."

"That's not necessary, Camille. I'm fine."

"No you're not," and she went to the phone and started dialing.

Next thing I know, I got a soft cast around my ankle and another lecture from this gal doctor who looked like she was still in high school and who I couldn't understand half of what she said.

She said something about needing to do an X-ray to make sure there was no damage to my brain when I fell.

"Do you understand?" she said to me.

I was about to say, *You the foreigner, what is it that I wouldn't understand?* but Camille jumped in and took over.

"She understands. I'll take her for the MRI from here and tomorrow we'll see a dentist."

The gal doctor put her hand on my shoulder.

"Okay, Mrs. Branch, you take it easy now. I'll see you back here in a few days."

Camille thanked her and I didn't say anything. I just wanted to get away from this candy striper as soon as possible.

"That wasn't so bad," Camille says as she helps me walk down the hall to the elevator.

"Speak for yourself."

"How're you feeling, Mom? Are you at all light-headed?"

"No, Camille, I'm fine. I told you that. Just take me home please so I can have my lunch and catch the rest of my stories."

"We still have to get the MRI, then we can go home. Do you need anything from the supermarket?"

"No, I just went yesterday. You know I always do my shopping on Thursdays."

"Okay, Mom. Well, I'm going to stay with you tonight and take you to Dr. Spain tomorrow."

"You don't have to stay with me. You can just pick me up in the morning. I'll be fine."

"I know, Mom, but I'll just be worrying so let me stay. Please?"

She was a persistent thing when she wanted to be.

"Fine."


## Camille

I hadn't stayed in my mother's house in more than twenty years. After I had Aisha my mother acted so ashamed I couldn't stand to be around her. Couldn't stand her or myself and I knew that wasn't good for Aisha. I knew that she'd somehow pick up on all of it and I just didn't want shame to be a part of her makeup. Even though Mom never said it, I knew how she felt, how I'd disappointed her, and I had enough of that stuff in the air, coming from strangers and people I knew. I didn't need it coming at me from my own mother.

The guest room hadn't changed. There was still the same patchwork quilt and rough green army blanket at the foot. The white lace curtains, the hickory pine furniture hadn't been moved or changed but was still immaculate. I pulled back the sheets and smelled that familiar Downy fresh smell. My mother kept her home Marthaesque correct. I welcomed the smell and looked forward to being here in my childhood home for one night.

I helped my mother into her nightgown and bed jacket when we got home and brought her lunch of soup and a tuna sandwich on a TV tray. She seemed to be relaxing and even smiled when she thanked me.

She liked her space, liked being alone, so I made sure not to crowd her. I left her alone until dinner, which I also brought into her bedroom.

She asked for a cup of tea with a shot of whiskey.

"These pills make me a little hyper," she said, when I looked at her funny for asking for whiskey.

"It'll help me sleep."

I brought it back and she dozed off watching *Wheel of Fortune*.

I set the cup and the shot glass on her nightstand and she woke up mumbling.

"Oh, Camille, what're you doing here?"

My heart stopped. I looked at my mother and reminded her that I'd been with her all day. She looked out the window and then back at me and nodded her head, of course. "I remember now. I fell."

I exhaled and said a silent thank you.

"Yes, Mom, and we have to get to the dentist tomorrow. *Do* you need anything?"

She straightened herself in bed and looked at the tea before taking the shot glass and hoisting it into her mouth like a coed doing tequila shots.

"Now I feel nice and warm. Is it warm enough in here for you?"

"Yes, Mom, I'm fine," I said, turning to walk out.

"Camille?"

I turned around.

"Why don't you stay and visit for a while," she said, patting a spot on her bed where she wanted me to sit.

I couldn't ever remember sitting on Mom's bed.

"It's alright. I've loosened up in my old age."

We smiled at each other and I sat down next to her on the bed.

"So what's going on?" she asked as she clicked off Vanna White.

"Well, work is busy as ever and I went to D.C.—"

"D.C.? For what?"

"Aisha's father died."

"That Morehouse boy, I thought he was from the midwest somewhere."

"Greg isn't Aisha's father. Aisha's father was a boy I knew at Lawrenceville. Adam, Adam Sorrell."

"Who the hell is Adam Sorrell?"

"You met him before. You and Daddy had come for parents' week, you only stayed for the day, but you met him."

"Lawd, you don't expect me to remember that? What, well, what happened?"

"He—It was drugs. He died of a drug overdose."

"My Lawd," she said, hand pressed to her chest. "Was he a colored boy?"

"Yes, he was Black. He was mixed actually, his mother is White."

"Ah, yes, I remember him. He had green eyes, I think, he was a nice fella, a little strange—"

"Yes, that was Adam."

"I thought he was decent."

"He was, Mom."

"Not if he was some old druggie. What in God's name—"

"People have problems Mom, they do all kinds of things to run away from them."

"Humph, what kind of problems could he have? A half-White boy with a rich man's education, please, Camille, save the bleeding-heart crap for somebody who deserves it, hear."

"Maybe that was part of his problem, you ever think of that?"

"What, lookin' White and being educated? No, that sounds like a pretty good hand to be dealt."

"Oh, I can't talk to you, I don't know why I bother." I got up to leave.

"Camille, don't leave. Please."

I looked at my mother and for the first time I saw the old woman she had become. She'd shrunk a little, her shoulders weren't nearly as broad as they once were, the skin hung a little from her face, but she still fixed herself up. Once a pretty woman. . . .

"I'm sorry to sound so harsh. You know how I am." She started to cry and stopped herself just as quickly.

I went to her and put my hand on her shoulder.

"Mom?"

She gathered herself back together, the formidable Geneva reappearing.

"It's just that Trudy's sick, and they think they got all the cancer out, but you know they can never be sure or if it's going to spread. . . ."

"Oh, Mom, I'm so sorry. Why didn't you tell me?"

"Ah, Trudy didn't want anybody to know till it was over."

"So where's she now?"

"She's with Herbie, in Connecticut. They're just gonna keep an eye on her. She's out of the hospital now."

My mother and Trudy have been friends since the Flood. Aunt Trudy was our godmother—mine and my brother's—and when we were little we knew that if something ever happened to Mom and Dad, Aunt Trudy would be the one to raise us.

"So how does she sound, you've talked to her?"

"Oh, of course, she sounds better every day, stronger, but you know Trudy keeps stuff so much to herself. She might know exactly what's happening but won't tell anybody."

"Even you?"

"Even me."

"It's what I was doing when I fell. I'd been on the phone with her, talking about the next trip we'd take when she's feeling better. We were laughing and carrying on. You know I didn't want to go back to Vegas, but she loved it there. I wanted to try one of those nice spas Oprah's always talking about. I'd stayed up later than usual and went in the bathroom to brush my teeth, that's when I blacked out."

"Well, we'll have to figure out a time when we can go see her."

"Yeah, 'cause she can't hide anything from me once I can look her in the eye."

I can just hear Aunt Trudy calling my mom VeVe. No one, not even my dad, ever called Mom anything other than Geneva, except Trudy.

"I'll call Herbie and figure out when would be a good time."

Mom patted me on the hand and I knew that meant she was pleased.

I got up to get myself something to eat.

"You want anything? I'm going to the kitchen."

"No, I'm fine but when you come back I want to hear more about Aisha's daddy."

I fixed myself a salad and a sandwich and brought it back into Mom's room on a TV tray; a TV tray that was older than me.

I told Mom about going to visit Adam's mother.

"Terrible thing to have to bury a child," she said, mostly to herself.

"She's a lovely person. I'm looking forward to having Aisha meet her, if she'll ever return my calls."

"You sure she want to meet her?"

Mom chewed a cracker on one side of her mouth, where her teeth were still intact.

"Of course she does. She can't wait. Why wouldn't she?"

"Well, you know some White folks ain't trying to claim their Black relatives."

"Yes, I suppose that's true of some, but Abby is hardly that. She was married to a Black man, for God's sake."

"Don't mean nothing—"

"You don't think her having a Black husband makes her less likely to be a racist?"

"Means the stuff was good and she decided she had to have it." Mom laughed and I joined her.

"You are so naughty."

"Yeah, but you know I'm right."

"Abby's not like that. You'll meet her. She's great."

Mom held out her shot glass and said whatever.

"Make it a sherry this time and get one for yourself. You need to lighten up."

I brought us each a glass of sherry. I never drink sherry, but it did have a way of making things seemed smoother.

"You know I love Trudy."

"Of course I know that, Mom. Where'd that come from?"

"She was with me when I met your daddy."

"I know, Mom."

"You know I loved him too."

"I know, Mom."

"I know you think I didn't love him, but I did, with all my heart, just like I loved you and MJ."

"I know that, Mom."

"Well, how come you were always criticizing me about how I used to talk to him? Always insinuating that I didn't love him or you."

"I don't remember doing that."

"You did it all the time."

"Well, maybe I did it because I didn't feel like you loved him or me. I know you were always so disapproving of me."

"What are you talkin' about?"

"Oh, Mom, you know what I'm talking about, especially after I had Aisha."

"Oh, chile, that's ancient history—but just for the record, once you had her I was only concerned about raising her the right way, helping you. I wasn't thinking about how she got here. She was here and we had to make sure that she was going to be alright."

I looked at my mother and she looked at me as if we were seeing each other for the first time in a very long time.

"You weren't ashamed of me all these years?"

"Ashamed? Maybe at first, when you told us you were pregnant, but hell, she was just about ready to come out at that point. After she was born all that mess got put away. You know I don't spend a whole lotta time looking backward."

"So I wasn't an embarrassment to you and all your friends?"

"What friends? Certainly not Trudy. You know she loved you like a daughter, anybody else who had a problem with my daughter wasn't no real friend of mine no how. I look at how you've raised that girl and I'm so proud of you. You did better than plenty of folks do with a husband."

"Well, I did have some help with Lem."

"Yes, you did, and you had the good sense to marry somebody like him."

"Don't tell me you're actually saying something nice about *the nappy-headed Negro from nowhere?*"

"Now what you talking about? I never said that, Camille."

"Mom, yes you did."

"Well, I don't recall. Lem is a wonderful man. You were foolish to break up with him. Daddy thought the world of him."

"How come neither of you ever said that?"

"What? Why did we have to? You know we weren't like that, going around talking about feelings all the time. You and MJ carry on like that, not us. Look, your dad and I were already outside because he was a musician, wasn't like anybody was expecting us to be like everybody else."

I felt tears welling up and turned to hug my mother. I held her tight to me and she, surprised at first, was limp in her return. When I didn't let go, she hugged me back hard.

"You don't know how long I wanted to hear you say this. I always wanted you to be proud of me."

"You're a hell of a person, Camille. How could you think otherwise?"

We weren't the hugging kind of family.

"Since it's truth-telling time, what do you think about Will?"

We looked at each other and laughed.

"You know that Daddy woulda had a fit."

"Yeah, I could just hear him now, *Aisha, have you lost all your marbles?*"

"I don't know, Mom, she seems happy, enough."

I added the "enough" because of the Miles part of the equation. I knew Mom didn't know about him and I wasn't about to be the one to tell her. Let Aisha tell her.

"Bull, I don't believe it and I'm not saying that just 'cause he's White. I don't think he's the right boy for her, he's too something, mamby-pamby."

"You think so? I don't really see that."

"Yes I do. He's not certain enough for our girl. She'll walk all over him and then you know she'll get bored, that seems to be genetic."

We'd never talked like this. I never knew my mother saw me the way she just said or that my parents had high regard for Lem. I did leave Lem out of boredom and now I was a little sorry about that. He was a good man and since him there's been nothing more than a few dates with men even more boring than he was.

"Yes, it's a curse, I'm afraid. We're just too quick."

"But you didn't feel that way about Daddy?"

"Nope, that's why I married him. I would've been bored to death if I'd married that fool from Hampton."

She finished off her sherry and asked for another.

"Mom, I don't think you should be drinking so much."

"Oh, Camille, stop acting like an old woman. I'm as healthy as you. Make it a double this time."

# CHAPTER 21

# The Black Swan

## *Aisha*

I woke up this morning to see the city below covered in snow. It was April and spring had officially begun.

*Sometimes the snow comes down in June, sometimes the earth goes round the moon, just when I thought our fates had passed you go and save the best for last . . .* I hear the lyrics in my head and wish I could sing them like Vanessa Williams. Yeah, sometimes it does snow in (practically) June. You weren't suppose to fall in love with someone else when you were about to get married, but sometimes you do. Mom had been trying to reach me and I knew I'd avoided her long enough. She was like a bloodhound in regard to my emotional life—she could just smell that something was up but this time I just had to figure this stuff out on my own. I decided to take one more day without talking to Mom, just flipping through magazines, giving myself a facial and lounging in my cashmere Juicy suit—which Will refers disparagingly to as my Bronx bombshell look.

"You sure it's not J-Lo?" he said, bopping his head and humming, *Don't be fooled by the rocks that I got, I'm still Jenny from the block, used to have a little now I got a lot.*

I could have a whole lot if I marry Will, but a lot of what?

I'd be the Black swan living the *Town and Country* life. I could have houses in several countries, a few continents. I could have a real Birken bag, and probably hand-me-down ones, which are even cooler; I could be *the* one in *W* and the other social rags; I could be on the junior benefit committees for the MET and ABT; I could be a regular in *Vogue* as one of those always chic women whose profession it is to be married into a wealthy family. That would be fun for about a minute, then I'd be bored outta my mind, looking around for something else, someone else who looks like me, needing to hang out in Harlem. I'm already tired of being the only one. It's like everybody notices you, can't help it 'cause you're the only one in the room, but they don't have to actually take the time to get to know you, to really see you. And the bitchy comments from these girls who haven't had to do anything on their own in their entire indulged lives—born on third and think they hit a triple. No, as much as I'd love to live la dolce vita, I know I'd get sick of it just as if I'd eaten too many sweets.

But what will I do? I'm running out of my severance and if I don't find another job soon I may have to *ohmygodperishthethought* move back in with my mother. Miles says I need to find my dad, that somehow that will clear my path. I don't know quite what he means, but I trust his advice. Miles seems to think all my restlessness has to do with the Daddy question. I don't know, but I guess it's worth a shot.

The snow was thick and annoyingly beautiful. We'd had seven storms this year, which has to be some kind of record. It was like the city was soundproofed and I loved that part. I walked to the newsstand for the papers, more fashion magazines, and to feel cold sunshine on my face. I wore my Uggs and loved the feeling of shearling against my bare feet. I stood at the corner newsstand flipping the glossy pages that were filled with images of models in bathing suits. As I was taking my time walking back, scanning faces in the crowd as I always do, it hit me. I was always looking, scanning; was I really in search of him, my daddy? I looked very little like my mom, more like Grandma but even that was a distant resemblance. My straight body was like none of the women on Grandma's side, they were all voluptuous, pear-shaped women; I had cheekbones like Mom before she gained so much weight that they had disappeared, but my nose, lips, eyes, whose were they?

I got back home and impulsively dialed Information for alumni affairs at Lawrenceville. I left a message and was promptly called back by someone who sounded like an NPR host. She was all soothing and brainy-sounding, efficient but not brusque.

"I'm so sorry to tell you that Adam Sorrell passed away last month. I can give you his mother's address if you'd like to send a note. . . ."

I was silent, trying to figure out what I was feeling.

"Are you a friend from school?"

"No, no. Thank you," I said, and hung up.

I stared at the phone, not knowing what to do. I should call Mom, but I didn't want her treating me like a baby or, worse, a client.

I called Miles on his cell.

"Where are you?"

He was skiing.

"I'm in Idaho. It's great. What's up, baby? You alright?"

Silence.

"Ish? What's wrong?"

I was crying and couldn't catch my breath.

"What happened? Calm down."

I told him the news.

"Damn, baby. I'm sorry. Did they say what happened?"

"No. I didn't ask."

"You talked to your mom? Maybe she knows something."

"Miles, I don't think it matters, at least to me."

"Why don't you come out here? Nothin' like skiin' down a mountain to clear shit up."

"I don't ski."

"Even better, you can learn somethin' new. It'll take your mind off things."

I sat here, looking out the window. The warmth of Saint Barts would be nicer right around here and I could see myself in one of those new Eres bathing suits, but I did need to jump outta here.

"Okay. I'll come."

"Cool. You may be able to get a flight out tonight, check American and you'll fly into Ketchum. I'll have a car pick you up at the airport and bring you to Sun Valley. Okay?"

"Okay."

"You cool?"

"I'm going to be. Thanks, Miles. I can't wait to see you."

"Me too, baby. Hang in there."

With that he hung up and I was grateful. I did what he said and got a flight.

I arrived early the next morning and was surprised that Miles was staying in a chalet on a slope that looked like something out of *Veranda*. He showed me around.

"Damn, Miles, this is bad."

"Yeah, it's a nice place."

"How'd you find it?"

"Oh, it belongs to a client—"

"Some client. Do all of them let you have their houses?"

"Well, you know, I make a little money for them, if I like them we become friends and you know friends help each other out. Here let me take that," he said, taking my tote from me and putting it in a pink and white Laura Ashley–style bedroom.

"If you don't like this one, you can move. There're are several others."

"So we're not staying in the same room?"

"It's the right thing to do, Ish, considerin' . . ."

"Miles, I'm here with you, we've already broken more than a few rules."

"I know, but, just, let's try to do this . . ."

"Okay, whatever you say. You're the boss."

He gave me a look, a smirk.

"Now you know and I know you know I know that ain't the truth."

I smiled and kissed him on the cheek.

Over a breakfast that he'd made of oatmeal, bacon, sausage and fruit, he told me that he'd enrolled me in a beginner's ski class. When I got there I found it was full of a bunch of rich brats. The oldest was nine. I imagined Will had been one of these kids who was probably skiing expertly by the time he was eight. He'd surely expect his children to do the same. I could care less.

I took my two-hour lesson and Miles met me afterward on the bunny slope as he said he would. After skiing together for several hours, me falling down only three times, Miles and I headed into the lodge for lunch; he was right about one thing—all the bright white snow and warm sun brightened me up right away.

By the end of the next day's lesson, I'd learned how to go

down some green trails mostly without falling. I felt five again—like I did when I spent all day playing outside, running, sweaty and happy or when Lem and I went on the father-daughter Jack and Jill ski trip together and went tubing.

It was one of the best times we'd ever had together with neither one of us knowing how to ski, but Daddy never left my side, always picking me up even though he could barely stand on the skis himself. It was around the time Cedra's father had bailed on her, after promising her that he'd be there. Her parents hadn't divorced yet, but her dad was already becoming more absent from her life.

"I really appreciate you inviting me, Miles," I said, over a lunch of hot dogs, burgers, french fries and milk shakes.

"It's cool. You always eat this much?"

"Uh-huh."

"How? Where does it go?"

"I don't know. I've always had this kind of metabolism. Look Miles, you don't have to stay with me on the bunny slopes. I know you want to get back to the bigger mountain."

"No, it's cool. I'm having fun watching you."

"Fall down."

He laughed, half covering his gap-toothed grin.

"I know how competitive you are. I know you wanna be out there doin' what, Blue trails? Blacks?"

"Ah, so you've been reading, I see."

"A girl's gotta stay informed."

"Well, for your information, I ski moguls."

"Of course you do."

Suddenly the lightness in Miles's face was gone, for a moment he looked stricken.

"Don't turn around now, but Garrison Fitzhugh is heading this way."

We were trapped. There was nowhere for me to run. I wouldn't even be able to climb under the table because of the pedestals and boots and jackets underneath—even if I were so inclined, which I was not.

"Just sit still, maybe he won't see us." Miles was now talking through a clenched smile.

Well, if he sees us, he'll save me the trouble, I think as I concentrate on sitting still, not turning until I see the back of him being trailed by a woman who was probably Will's age, dressed in a white Chanel down jacket and a fake fur scrunchie holding up her perky blonde ponytail.

"Small world," Miles said, shaking his head. "Damn, that was fucked up."

I said nothing for a few minutes.

"Well, what do you wanna do now?" he asked.

"Could we go back to the house and make a fire?"

He grinned and said add a brandy and that would be perfect.

The fireplace was built into the stone wall that reached through the second story and went out through the roof.

Miles put in the logs, concentrating like a boy at a troop outing. I made a brandy Alexander for me and gave him his straight, the way he wanted it.

We sat next to each other on the floor, our backs leaning against the sofa, facing the fire.

"Mm, this is good. You wanna taste?"

"Is it sweet?"

"Yes . . ."

"I don't like sweet and alcohol."

"Oh, taste it."

He took it from my hand and tasted it and smiled.

"That is pretty good. Like a milk shake with nutmeg . . ."

"And brandy."

"Whatever."

"So, that was pretty wild today, huh?"

"Yup. It's a sign. You shouldn't be creepin' around 'cause there's always somebody who knows you."

"So you've never cheated before?"

"I always tell the truth."

"So you've never cheated on a girlfriend?"

"I always told the truth. If I was creepin' she knew about it. If I said I wasn't, I didn't."

"Always, Miles?"

"Pretty much. I mean, I ain't counting college and there was one time. It was a situation like this, where she was seeing someone else, but she used to be my girlfriend. . . ."

"And what happened?"

"She and I were having dinner and her dude just like busted in the restaurant, came over to our table like John Wayne and . . . I just left."

"So why am I here with you?"

He finished his brandy and put the snifter on the floor.

He looked into my eyes.

"I think we both know there's something big going on here."

We kissed each other and I didn't sleep in the pink and white Laura Ashley bedroom that night.

# CHAPTER 22

# Can't Miss What You Never Had

"I was wondering when in the hell you were going to call. Where've you been? And why didn't you tell me you lost your job? And—"

"Mom, Mom, slow down. Can I get a word in?"

"Aisha, don't you dare use that tone with me, like I'm the one out here acting like I've lost my mind."

"Mom, I didn't get fired, the firm merged and I got a decent severance package. I'm sorry I haven't been in touch. I've just been going through a lotta stuff and for once I'm trying to work it out on my own."

"Okay, look I have something to tell you," Mom says.

I could hear it in her voice. The grave sound, but not too grave because after all she is the mommy and she doesn't fall apart. She can't so that I can.

"Mom, I already know."

"Know what?"

"That my real dad died."

"How'd you know?"

"I had decided that I needed some closure with him, so I called Lawrenceville to get his number and, well, they told me."

I could hear my mom sigh.

"I'm okay, Mom, really."

"So you're fine? You've worked everything all out?"

"Well . . ."

I told her about Miles and the ski trip.

"*Whhhaaat*— you ran into the father? How's that for bad luck? What'd he say? What'd you do?"

"Well, he didn't see us—"

"You hope."

"Doesn't matter, 'cause I told Will. We broke up last night, when I got back. I'm meeting him later and I'll give him the ring back."

"So did you tell him about Miles? What'd you say?"

"I told him that he was a great guy but I didn't think we had enough to make a marriage work, not like I want a marriage. I told him that I'd been attracted to Miles, but that that wasn't the reason that I was breaking up with him."

"What'd he say?"

"He didn't say much, other than I understand. Frankly, he didn't seem all that upset, I have to say, but you know what, that's part of the problem. I just can't get to him, he's so repressed, so removed, so infinitely polite. I don't want that."

"Well, good for you, baby. I'm proud of you."

"You are? You don't think I'm a total fuck-up?"

"Nope. I think you're brave."

"You do?"

"When all this blows over, I want to take you to meet your grandmother, she's dying to meet you."

"Where?"

"D.C. I'm sorry you had to find out like that. That's why I've been trying to reach you."

"It's okay. You can't miss what you never had."

"Well, I went down there and she's a wonderful woman. Adam was her only child, and you're her only grandchild."

"Mom, I'm kinda tired now. I want to go to bed."

Even though I was being stoic, I knew Mom understood that I just needed to curl up in my bed and pull the shades. I'd been though a lot in the past few weeks.

"I just have to get through one thing at a time."

"Yes, sweetheart. You just need closure with Will. . . ."

"Ma!"

"What?"

"Stop talking to me like a shrink! How many times do I have to tell you that?"

"I'm sorry. You're right. Rest up, talk to Will and I'll speak with you tomorrow."

There was no easy way to do this, so I figured I'd keep it simple and make it quick.

Will and I met at a frill-free coffee shop—you know, the kind where the waitresses call you hon and look like they all keep Aqua Net in business. I arrived first, figuring the least I could do was not make him wait to get his humiliation.

He was wearing a shabby brown corduroy jacket, no doubt from his Andover days, and looked as if he hadn't slept or bothered to comb his hair when he slumped into the booth, barely looking at me.

I wondered if his dad had seen me with Miles and if he'd told him about the sighting but didn't dare ask him. It didn't matter now, anyway. It was done.

"Will, I just want to say—"

"Aisha, don't say anything, just give me the ring and I'll leave."

He didn't sound hostile, just tired.

"I'm really sorry."

"For which thing, being a slut or blowing me off?"

He now looked at me, daring me to say something to contradict him.

I reached across the table to caress his hand, but he snatched it away.

"I don't need to hear how sorry you are."

He got up from the booth and stuck out his hand.

I put the ring in his palm.

"Where's the watch?"

"Oh, I'm sorry, I forgot. I'll have it sent over."

I had stopped wearing it a few weeks ago and had put it away.

"I'll send a messenger to get it later."

"Will . . . I didn't want to be your dusky exotic."

"Oh, Aisha, get off the race shit. It's tired and nobody wants to hear about it."

I watched Will walk out, pushing the door harder than he needed, probably imagining it was my face. And it was over. I sat at the booth for a while longer, trying to figure out how I felt.

When I got home there was another message from Daddy. When I heard his voice I knew it was Lem, my Daddy, but it was weird that when he said, "it's Daddy" on the message for a moment I thought somehow my real Dad had somehow called me. Lem was the only Daddy I'd ever known but suddenly I was thinking about someone I'd never met and I suddenly felt a pang of loss for what I didn't have, a relationship with the person who was biologically responsible for me being here. Daddy's tone was all concerned which only means Mom told him about my real dad dying.

I plopped down on the sofa and dialed his number.

"How's my baby girl?" he said once his secretary got him on the line.

"Hey, Dad, you busy?"

"You know I'm never too busy for my baby girl. I called you."

"I know. I'm calling you back."

"Aisha, that was days ago."

"I've been away."

"I heard. Is everything okay? You need anything?"

"I'm okay, just trying to figure out what to do with my life."

"You okay with money, you need a little something? Need to go shopping?"

"Daddy, come on, of course I always need a little something."

"Done. I'll have something put into your account today. You sure you're alright? Mom told me about you and Will."

Now this was a shock. Daddy never, ever wanted to talk about anything intimate. He'd just as soon pretend he didn't know about such things.

"I'm fine, Daddy."

I didn't feel like discussing Will with him and I'm sure he really didn't want any details.

Let mom tell him, which I'm sure she would eventually, if she hadn't already.

"Okay then. I've gotta be in court in a few minutes. Love you, baby."

"Thanks, Daddy. Love you too."

I hung up and smiled at the phone. I couldn't have made

up a sweeter daddy. My mom was a fool to leave him; so what
if he's a little boring. He's the best daddy a girl could ever
want.

As much as I knew I could just get money from him and
not really have to work for several months, I wanted to find
something to do. Having too much free time wasn't good for
anybody, especially me.

I needed talk to my grandma.

She was nicely recovered from her fall. She had a bridge for
where she'd lost two teeth and there hadn't been any other
damage. I called her like I usually did after Oprah. I wanted to
tell her myself about my breakup with Will.

"Well, how're you feeling about it?" she asked, coming back
to the phone after shutting off the local news. I could hear her
shuffling to the phone, mumbling to herself about how she
"can't stand that noise." She despised local news with all their
reports of baby snatchings and pit bull killings. "It's just foolishness," Grandma would rant.

"So, you doing okay, baby?"

"I'm fine, Grandma, how're you doing?"

"Oh, I'm just fine. You know Trudy's not doing so hot."

"Yes, Mommy told me. Did you have a nice visit?"

"Yes, we did. Janice, that's Herbie's wife, always makes such
a fuss. She made us a nice lunch and served us out in the garden. It was just lovely."

"So, Mom said Aunt Trudy's lost a lot of weight."

"Yes," Grandma sighed, "she doesn't look good. But how
you doing, baby? You and your fella broke up?"

"Yeah, it wasn't right for me."

"I know. I knew that from the time I laid eyes on him."

I wanted to laugh but I knew Grandma was straight-up
serious.

"What did you see?"

"Well, I didn't think he'd keep your interest. You know what I mean?"

"Yes, Grandma, I know what you mean."

"Now who's this new one?"

Damn, Mom, can't you keep anything to yourself, I thought.

"Well, I'll bring him over, let you check him out."

"Tell me somethin' about him. Where his people from? What kind of work does he do?"

"He's from Memphis. His folks are all pretty much from Tennessee, but his mother just passed away. . . ."

"Oh, that's too bad. He got brothers and sisters?"

"No, he's an only child."

"Like you. Where's his daddy?"

"Well, he died a few years ago, but he wasn't around."

"Mmm, so you both were brought up with just your mamas—"

"Yeah, that's right, until Mom married Daddy. Miles didn't have a stepfather."

"It's hard for women with boys."

I knew this was another of Grandma's views on the world and wasn't up for that conversation. I changed the topic from Miles.

We talked more about her garden, church and Oprah—I told her that I couldn't stop thinking about those Ethiopian women and the fistulas.

"Well, you know what that means? The Lord is trying to tell you something."

"Like what? You wanna interpret?"

We both laughed easily as we always did.

"I'm thinking about doing more than just sending money."

"Well, baby, just pray on it, He'll tell you what to do."

Before hanging up, I promised to bring Miles as soon as the time was right.

I hung up and realized how lucky I was to still have her, realizing that when her time came, I wouldn't be ready.

# CHAPTER 23

# Say It to Me in French

I hadn't talked to Miles since we'd come back from the trip. I didn't want him to feel crowded but I called him and tried to act cool.

"I'm looking for a job. You have any leads?"

"What kind of job?"

"Right now I just need something to do, I want to eventually do something in fashion, maybe magazines."

"Well, I don't know anybody in that world, but you could come work for me."

"Work for you? Doing what?"

"You could be a hostess at one of the restaurants, just until you figure out your next move."

I pictured the women who do this at restaurants around the city and they are always attractive and usually very thin.

"Yeah, I could do that. What do I have to do?"

"Well, you're on your feet a lot, all day really. You take reservations, escort people to tables, make sure the wait staff is assigned to the right areas, that's pretty much it."

"What's the money like?"

"It stinks, but you can make decent tips and you'll meet a lot of people, maybe you'll meet somebody in magazines."

My gears were really turning now.

"Yeah, okay, I'm interested. What do I do?"

"You should come down to Maya and meet my partner and the staff and we'll go from there. Come tomorrow, around eleven."

"Cool. Thanks, Miles."

"No problem."

Was it my imagination or was Miles being a little cool to me? I'm sure he's not happy about Garrison knowing that his friend was seeing his son's fiancée, but Garrison and Miles continued doing business together. Just business, it's not personal.

The next day I arrive at Maya in my new Pucci shirt, a Dolce and Gabbana green skirt with purple stripes and dark cherry suede sandals, determined to play it cool with Miles, like, *Look, I'm a grown-up too and I'm not going to pressure you.* Miles was seated in a corner banquette along with three other people. He waved me over and I smiled and greeted everyone.

I sat down and they all looked at me, the guy poured me a cup of coffee. He was foreign, couldn't tell what, German? Swedish? He had that Continental quality that just seemed more polished than a regular old American. When he spoke he had an accent, but his English was flawless. He was Miles's partner, Bernhard.

"So, Aisha, what kind of work have you been doing?" he asked.

"I was, until recently, an assistant media buyer, at Rowe."

"Ah, yes, I've heard of them. And you didn't like the job?"

"Well," I looked at Miles and he nodded at me, as if to say, *Tell the truth, be yourself.*

"No, I didn't. I want a little more creativity and a lot less paperwork."

Everyone laughed.

The woman who was the manager spoke.

"Well, the restaurant business seems glamorous but it's a lot of work. How do you respond to pressure? You've got two couples standing before you, a guy hovering for his table and the phone is ringing, what do you do?"

"Well, I'd tell the person on the phone that I'd be with them shortly. I'd suggest that the guy hovering step to the bar, that a choice table is being cleared, and then I'd deal with the two couples. I'd size them up, if they were young and from the city I'd give them a little attitude, 'cause they'd expect it, if our place is hot, then I should give them just a little bit of 'tude. If they were older and from the suburbs I'd be nicer to them and have them wait at the bar."

They all looked at one another, pleased with my answer.

"Bravo, Aisha." Bernhard gave Miles a nod, who said to me that they needed to confer and suggested I give them a minute.

"Sure, I'll just . . ."

"We won't be long. Go have a pastry, John's making up something fresh in the back," Miles said.

I went to the ladies' room, checked my hair, put on more lip gloss and then went out and drank a cup of tea with a piece of flaky apple something that was so good I wanted to lick the plate. Miles came back and got me, just before I'd resorted to sucking my fingers. I sat there, looking around the walnut walls and floors, the burnished silver accents, and realized I didn't want this. I'm not the hostess type, although I easily could play the part, but doing so would be ignoring a huge part of me, just like marrying Will would've done the same thing. I don't want to be some thing, even if it's some exotic beautiful thing. I'm not an object like a damn Ming vase. I'd rather work in a McDonald's than shimmy in a tight dress and heels every night leading diners like unsuspecting sheep to their overpriced dinners. Oh God, am I becoming my mother?

Miles came and joined me at the small round table.

"Congratulations. You're hired," he said, sitting down.

"Really? Oh, thanks, Miles." I looked down the restaurant to see if the others were still sitting there.

"You were really good, better than I even expected and I expected that you'd be good."

"I'm gonna pass."

Miles looked at me, his eyebrows raised, and waited.

"I just don't want you helping me like this, it feels weird. It's like either we're having a relationship as equals or you're going to take me on as some kind of protégée. I'm not interested in the latter. And I'm just not a hostess."

"I just . . ." he said.

"I know, you were just trying to help me and I'm touched by your effort, but really, I'll find something on my own."

He shrugged and said okay, but I know he was still confused.

"Miles, I want to be with you. I've said that over and over and you remain elusive. I realize this whole thing with Will and his father being your friend . . ."

He put his two fingers across my lips.

"Hush. I'll call you later and we'll talk, okay?"

I smiled at him and agreed. I walked to the front and thanked his partner and the manager for their time and left.

I walked out to Union Square where the farmers' market was set up and walked around smelling the herbs and flowers and fresh fruit brought in from outlying farms. Finally you could actually smell and feel spring. I felt my own budding promise and felt happy.

My cell rings as I pay for some cucumbers. It's Miles.

"I didn't know you meant ten minutes," I said.

"Meet me for lunch?"

"Sure. Where?"

"Tocqueville."

"Why so special?"

"'Cause you are."

I walk the one block east to the one-tiny-room underground restaurant that smells of fresh freesia. A record of a Frenchwoman singing softly is playing in the background and I'm glad that I look casually, perfectly turned out, like the French. My hair is not blown out but curly and loose, which makes me look more exotic. My Pucci shirt, little slim-to-the-knee skirt and my Jimmy Choos make me feel oh so French.

*"Bonjour,"* the maitre d' says.

*"Le bon après-midi, comment sont vous."*

*"Très bon, merci."*

He shows me to the table. He treats me as if I'm a regular. I get through with enough *très biens* and *ouis* that my stock is high.

Miles arrives and I see the greeting they gave me was nothing. They treat him like the damn sultan has arrived home. Two ridiculously chic women having lunch are openly staring at us. One woman looks vaguely familiar, but is wearing large oval-shaped tinted glasses.

After a few cheek kisses with the maitre d' and a waiter, Miles sits next to me and kisses me on one cheek.

"You smell good. So, what looks good?"

"I've studied the menu and decided on a nice piece of lamb, french fries and appetizer of mussels in butter and wine."

"Sounds perfect. I'll have the same thing."

Miles's phone rings and he puts his finger up as he answers. It's not business and after a few seconds I detect that it's a woman. A first in all the times I've been with him. He talks pleasantly for a few minutes before telling his caller that he's having lunch.

He laughs, I hear him say, "A friend, yes, she's female." He winks at me.

He gets off and puts the phone on vibrate before putting it in the inside pocket of his blazer.

"Now," he says, taking my hand in his, "where were we?"

"So how many women are in love with you? I realize we've never had this conversation and while you were on the phone I was sitting here thinking I should ask."

"Ish, come on, baby. Let's order some delicious food, have some nice wine and enjoy."

The waiter arrived with a bottle, presented it to Miles, who nodded and held up his goblet.

The waiter poured and waited. Miles sipped and nodded. The sultan had been doing this for a very long time.

"I am enjoying. It's just a question. What are there, three, four, five, a hundred?"

He laughed.

"Ish, a hundred?"

"Miles, I'm all about you, have been since we met and I know you're into me too. I just want to know as much about you as I can."

"Let me just tell you this, I'm with you and there's no place else I want to be."

He holds up his glass.

"To spring."

I clink and eye him suspiciously.

"To spring."

We were on to sharing a lovely chocolate soufflé when the two chic women stopped at our table on their way out.

"*Excusez-moi*, we couldn't help noticing you," the younger of the two said.

Miles and I looked at her and then the other, who was wrapped in a sea-green cashmere shawl. She half smiled but said nothing. The younger one handed me her card.

"You have incredible style and we're working on a new project that I'd love for you to give me a call."

I read her card: FASHION EDITOR FRENCH VOGUE.

"I'm here till next week."

I looked up at her and realized that I'd seen her picture in all the fashion trades, always seated in the front row of the big fashion shows.

"Sure. *Je vous appellerai demain*," I say, trying not to leap on her and tell her I'd work for her for free.

"*Bon*. I'll look forward to it. Isn't the food *divine? A toute à l'heure.*"

"*A toute à l'heure. Merci beaucoup.*"

With that they gave us toothless smiles and left.

"Miles, can you believe this."

"You speak French well."

"Ah, *un peu.*"

"Well, it's turning me on. Let's have a little coffee back at my apartment."

"It's two in the afternoon."

"I know. You gotta be someplace?"

"I guess not."

Back at Miles's apartment we go at like we did the first time we were together, starting in the elevator.

"You look so damn hot in that skirt," he said, as we stood next to each other in the elevator, his hand rubbing my thigh.

Inside the apartment, he put his hands inside my shirt and we kissed deeply.

"I want you so bad."

He pushed off my shrug and I unbuttoned my blouse, squeezed out of my skirt and stood before him in bra and panties.

"I love you, Miles," I said, before unzipping his pants and pushing him toward the sofa.

I kissed him and kept kissing him. I didn't want him to think about what I'd just said, didn't want him to feel like he had to say it back.

I pleasured him, as I knelt in front of him and he ran his fingers through my hair. What I lacked in experience, I'd make up for with enthusiasm.

We ended up asleep in the bed, unaware of the outside world, until it was dark outside. He shook me awake, saying that he needed to check in at the restaurants.

"You want me to go with you?"

"No, you don't have to. Why don't you stay here and relax. I'll be back in a couple hours. I'll bring dinner."

"Only if we can eat it in bed . . ."

"Absolutely." With that he kissed me and went to shower and dress.

I went back to sleep.

I had a dream that I told Miles about my father and he reacted negatively when I told him that my biological father had been half-White. I woke up confused about whether it had actually happened or it was a dream.

I didn't want to go back to sleep because I didn't want to dream anymore. I decided to give in to something I knew I shouldn't but couldn't help myself. Once I went through his freezer, eating the chocolate brownie Ben & Jerry's, the only thing there, I went into his study, stood there, trying to decide where he might keep his phone book. He didn't seem like a journal keeper, but wouldn't it be great if he were, if I could find it.

*Stop,* I hear my mother and Cedra in my head. *He likes you, you're crazy about him, don't do it.* I stood in the doorway a little longer before I let myself obey. Just then the phone rang— should I answer it? He would just call me on my cell if he needed to speak to me. It rang, I'm sure he had one of those phone answering systems, oh, but what about caller ID, I could look to see without answering, that was harmless enough. So, I went to the phone to see, sure enough, it was a woman, a Lisa Ondosdi. The TV news anchor? I didn't dare pick up the phone, as much as I wanted to; but what would he do? Would he tell me he never wanted to see me again? Over that? He might. He didn't say not to answer the phone, but it is kind of an unwritten rule when you're anything less than engaged. So, I let it go, let Lisa Ondosdi leave her message.

Pictures, that's harmless enough. He had leather-bound and dated photo albums lined up on a bookcase shelf in his den. I curled up in his leather armchair with one. There was Miles wearing a lopsided Afro and infamous shit-eating grin, graduating from college with I guess his mother next to him wearing the identical smile and a flowered dress. Even their eyes are smiling. Another was of Miles with a woman who looked ordinary-pretty like that model Veronica Webb, at what looked like a formal affair, maybe a wedding. She had that hopelessly-in-love look in her eyes and he just looks uncomfortable; there's another with a woman with a lot of reddish brown Diana Ross–type hair, big pretty lips in a funky sexy outfit. They have similar seductive grins and seem like two of a kind. Why am I doing this to myself? I know he's got all kinds of choices, woman hurling themselves at him to be number two or three, forget number one, and I have the nerve to want it all.

I decided to call the woman from *French Vogue* tomorrow. I need a job and a Miles distraction. I felt I was on the way to being obsessed with him and if there's any way to kill one's chances with a man it is to be a tiny bit obsessive. He was too smart to go for the playing-it-cool way, but I can really be cool, really be preoccupied if I were to get with *French Vogue*.

Miles came back in exactly two hours with lobster in a creamy sauce with pasta, broccoli rabe and ricotta cheesecake with fresh strawberries.

"You know how to spoil a girl," I said, inhaling my food.

"I hope you're not too hungry. I tried to be as fast as I could."

"I ate your Ben & Jerry's."

"That's all? So how much of my stuff did ya go through?"

"Miles," I said in my best Scarlett.

"Ish. I've been around for a long time, sweetheart."

"I just looked at a photo album."

"Ah-ha. Anything interesting?"

"Well—"

"Ask away . . ."

"I can?"

"Sure. I'm not into secrets."

"Who's the one with the reddish hair? You two looked happy."

"Which book?"

I pointed to the one I'd looked at, the forest-green leather one, which I'd left on the coffee table.

"Oh, let's see, that was three years ago. That's Natasha, the one I was engaged to."

"Oh, she's pretty. Where's she now?"

"In L.A. She's a movie producer."

"She looks like somebody."

"Yeah, she's good people. You'd like her."

Mmm.

"What about this one?" I got up to point out the one in formal wear.

"Ah, that's Alice. Alice Andrews."

He was silent for a moment, obviously reliving some long-ago memory.

"So, what happened with her?"

"That one was a long time ago, about ten years. I loved her, but our timing was off."

"What d'you mean?"

"I was too young. She wanted to settle down, I just wasn't ready."

"You were thirty-three ten years ago."

"Yeah, so, and I wasn't ready."

"Where's she now?"

"I don't know. She got married, has a couple kids. I've lost touch with her."

"What did she do?"

"She was a journalist."

"Do you date any underachievers?"

He laughed out loud.

"It's not a requirement. Just turns out that way, I guess. I like smart women who like to mix it up."

"Is that what you really like, or what you want in the press release?"

"Ah, that's a very good question, my dear. I think I straight-up like smart people, period. You've gotta be able to get the ball back over the net, but of course, the problem comes in when it gets serious and the conversation about who's gonna take care of the babies comes and—"

"Natasha didn't want to stay home?"

"Naw, well, she said she wanted to, but I knew that wasn't true or that it wouldn't be right for her to give up all she'd worked for. I'd feel too guilty about that . . . but that was then."

"So is that why you broke up?"

"Probably . . . Not really."

I looked at him, clearly confused.

"I mean if I'd really loved her, I would've married her. We would've figured out the rest."

"So you didn't?"

"Not as much as I wanted to."

"Well, that's very honest of you."

"So, any more questions?"

"No, but you did have a phone call."

"Who was it?"

"I didn't answer your phone."

"You could've."

"Really?"

"I told you, I ain't got nothin' to hide."

"So you still haven't answered one question."

"Which one?"

"So how many are there?"

"Oh, but I did. Perhaps you didn't understand. There are other women that I date, but right now I'm enjoying you."

"So how come you haven't settled down with somebody? I mean Natasha was three years ago, what are you waiting for?"

"Kismet."

I held out my glass for more wine.

"Kismet, huh."

"Yeah, like today. How's that for kismet, meeting the woman from *Vogue?* I hope it works out for you, baby."

I nodded, said me too and drank my wine.

# CHAPTER 24

# Oui Kismet

It was certainly kismet for me meeting Martine Philippe, the French editor-in-chief of *French Vogue*. Martine told me about their plans to start a new magazine. Something edgy, something ethnic and they wanted to hire me as a stylist, maybe eventually becoming some kind of editor. First they'd need me to freelance on the first trial issues, show me the ropes.

She'd later tell me that she was immediately attracted by my style and beauty. Martine grew up in Mozambique with her beautiful, depressed French mother and Portuguese physician father; she went to Swiss and American boarding schools.

"Asha," she'd taken to pronouncing my name, "you are very beautiful. I know this is not a gift."

No one had ever said that to me before. How had she read something so profound about me after knowing me only minutes? Was it forecast on me somehow?

"I hope you will bring all of your *experience de la vie* to this project, a *perspective unique sur* beauty."

I just looked at her, nodding, wondering what she saw in me, wondering what kind of powers she had, or was she merely perceptive? She told me I'd travel to Paris in the next few weeks for the fashion shows.

"It will be, how you say, *epreuve sous le feu?* Trial of under fire, *oui.*"

I was trying to translate in my head before she did it for me.

"Ah, a trial under fire."

"I adore the way you dress. This is exactly what we want for the pages, more individuality, more, how you say? Funk."

I wanted to laugh at the way she pronounced *funk,* but I also wanted to kiss her for being able to see me. I always knew I had an unusual sense of style but mostly I often just got made fun of . . . I loved shopping in Grandma's attic and vintage shops. I was dressed in my favorite vintage black and brown Chanel jacket, bought at a flea market in Georgia when I was in high school, off-white corduroys, my red Jimmy Choo sandals and a fuchsia and black striped T-shirt.

"I love what you're wearing."

"Ah, it's ancient Comme des Garçons. Such a talent," she said, smoothing down the fitted black riding jacket worn over pipe-leg pants and high-heeled sandals with bare feet.

"I've always loved putting seemingly disparate pieces together, couture and Target," I said.

Martine's face lit up.

"Ah, *oui,* exactly, that is what we want for this new venture. I know this is difficult, because we cannot officially offer you a job until we see if it takes off, but we'd like for you to work on the mock-up."

I wasn't doing anything else, but knew enough not to tell this to Martine.

"When can you start?"

And I thought, Like yesterday.

I handed her my résumé, which she seemed to do no more than glance at and instructed me where to go to get a temporary ID and to give them my Social Security number.

"You'll start fresh on Monday, *oui?*"

"*Oui.*"

She took me around, showing me the tiny space and introducing me to about a dozen people who made up this still unnamed, unformed *French Vogue* offshoot.

"Obviously, most of our people are in France. This is more, how you say, an outpost?"

"Yes," I said, nodding my head.

"Asha, I'm so pleased we met." She stuck out her hand.

"I will see you Monday."

I didn't really know what time and hated to have to bog her down with such boring details.

"Ah, yes, be here by ten."

She walked me to the door, put her hand on my shoulder, we Euro air-kissed and I left.

I went home and found messages from my mom saying that my newfound grandmother Abby would be coming to town this weekend to see me. She couldn't wait any longer for me to get to D.C. "She's dying to meet her grandchild," my mom said on the message. I didn't know how I felt about meeting Abby, this stranger who was also my grandmother. I didn't feel bad, but I wasn't all that looking forward to it either. I'd hoped to be able to put it off until I figured out how I felt.

There was also a message from Will, he sounded drunk, like he was calling from a bar.

"Ash, it's me, Will, I'm sitting here with Paul and Chop and feeling like shit and I wanna talk to you. I need to talk to you. . . . Call me when you get this."

I didn't want to talk to him but I did realize after hearing his voice that I missed him, a little. I missed his puppy-dog worship even though it was misplaced. Everyone likes feeling adored, don't they?

I plopped on my bed, in my tiny studio apartment, happy for my fluffy flannel comforter that Grandma had given me for Christmas. I would just hang out here till I had to see Abby tomorrow for lunch. I watched TV, checked in with Cedra:

"So, what's up? Haven't heard from you since the exam. How was it?"

"It's over. I won't get the results for another week," she said.

"What were you doing?"

"Just reading, I was out all day, I'm tired."

"You sound funny. Are you pissed at me?"

"Ash, I . . ."

"What? Just say it. You don't have to mince words with me, come on. . . ."

"I'm just having a hard time here. First you meet fabulous Will and now there's even more fabulous Miles. I can't even get a fucking date."

I looked at the phone. Like maybe I'd misdialed and got someone who was not my best friend, Cedra.

"And you feel like how come I have—"

"Everything, yes, that's how I feel. Like you get the great looks, and the rich stepdaddy—"

"Please, you know Lem is hardly rich."

"Rich in the world we come from. I know things haven't been easy for you, but—"

"Whoa, easy. What the fuck. Don't tell me you're hating now, not you, not my girl Cedra."

"Ash, I could never hate on you. I love you and you know that, but I'm not gonna front, I'm not feeling you right now. Okay. I said it. You have everything, you always did. Even when we were little and both of our parents were getting divorced. Yours was a civilized one; mine was all crazy."

Cedra stopped herself.

"Well, I'm surprised to hear you say this. I don't know how to respond."

"I don't know either. I haven't called because I didn't want to have this conversation. I wanted these feelings to just go away...."

"But I knew something was up. Didn't you know I'd know?"

"Yeah, I know. Look, this will pass, just like when you got your advance Brownie badge and I didn't."

I had to laugh at that memory.

"Okay? We okay?" she said, sounding contrite.

"Yeah. Sure. I've gotta go."

"Sure. Let's talk again. I'll call you in a few weeks."

"Okay."

I sat and looked out of the window. I couldn't believe what Cedra had said. I knew she was pissed at me, she'd been acting weird forever, but I never expected all that. How was I supposed to respond to my best friend being jealous of me—even though I had the feeling that she was, I was hoping that I was wrong; this was not like when we were in Brownies or even Jack and Jill. We were grown women now and we both needed to know who we could trust. How could she be jealous of me anyway? She was the one with the serious work that she loved and was good at. She didn't seem to really want a boyfriend because if she did she could have one. There were guys who liked her; she was just too damn picky. She wouldn't even discuss going out with White guys; she wouldn't go out with anyone who wasn't at least several inches taller than her and she's five eight. She didn't like fraternity guys, guys who weren't athletic or men who didn't like going to art museums.

I decided to just return Will's call.

He answered on one ring.

"Hey, how are you?"

"I'm good. I got your message."

"Yeah, I was kinda hammered."

"I could tell."

"I mean, but I meant what I said."

Silence.

"You there?"

"I'm here."

"Look, I love you and I want to try again. I know I was stupid, always groping you and whatnot. I shouldn't have done that. . . ."

"And calling me a slut . . ."

"I know, I'm so sorry."

"Will, it's not about that."

"So what is it about?"

"I just . . ."

"What, you don't miss me?"

"I do, but—"

"But what? What's the problem? Just let me come over."

I knew I shouldn't have, but he sounded so pathetic I didn't have the heart to say no.

As I sat dreading, waiting for him to come over I remembered when he proposed. We were on the Staten Island ferry and I was eating a hot dog. He liked to ride the ferry back and forth. It was something he used to do when he was in elementary school; before his parents divorced; before boarding school; before he knew who he was supposed to be. It was where he'd been the happiest.

We'd only been dating about a year. We were having fun, I liked him a lot, but had no idea he was this serious. We're on the ferry, the summer breeze making me feel just like that Isley Brothers song . . . *summer breeze makes me feel fine blowing through the jasmine in my mind.* Will dabs his napkin on the mustard I had on the corner of my mouth and takes a swig of beer that he's smuggled on. He gets down on a knee and I'm thinking he's dropped something. He takes my hand, looks me in the eye very seriously and says, "Aisha, I love you, I think you know that."

"Will, what are you doing?"

"Can you be quiet?" He takes out a velvet box and opens it.

"I want to marry you. Will you be my wife?"

I swallow a chunk of hot dog and put my hand over my wide-opened mouth, to keep from screaming, I think. I look at him, look at the ring, the most brilliant diamond, a massive cushion cut, and I think, What the hell is going on? I had one of those out-of-body things, where you can stand over yourself and watch yourself.

I stare at him, on his knee, looking so goofy.

"Get up, please."

"Not until you answer me."

"Yes. Yes, I'll marry you."

He got up and we hugged each other. He slipped the ring onto my finger.

We hugged.

\* \* \*

I opened the door and there he was standing with a bunch of pale yellow tulips wrapped in a blue ribbon.

"They're so pretty. Thank you," I said, moving out of the doorway for him to come in. "You want something to drink? A soda?"

"Naw, I'm cool."

We sat on the sofa, which was on the opposite wall from my bed; a TV on a bookcase created two areas of my studio.

He looked around, as if seeing the place for the first time. We never spent time here. He was probably thinking, How does she live in this tiny ass space?

I liked it just fine. I guess the way my mom liked her little crooked house.

It's mine.

"So, what you been up to?"

"I got a new job."

"Word. Where?"

"Well, it's kind of a freelance thing. *French Vogue* is starting a new magazine and I'm going to be a stylist."

"Really, Ash, that's dope, congratulations. I know you love all that fashion stuff."

*That fashion stuff?*

"I do. I'll get to go to Paris, go to the shows. I'm really amped."

Amped? I never say that stupid word. Whenever I was around Will and his friends I'd morph into talking their combination preppy hip-hop slang.

I shuddered to think what else I'd morphed into without realizing it.

"So, I got something of a promotion."

"Oh yeah? Art director?"

"Yup. Got an office, an assistant. It's pretty cool, I guess."

"An office, that's big."

"So, Ash, what do you think? You wanna try it again?"

"Will, I don't know."

"Are you seeing somebody?"

"Well, sort of."

"Who, Miles?"

"Yes, Will. I'm seeing Miles."

He looked stung even though he already knew the answer.

"We don't need to have this conversation, Will."

"Why are you being all formal? What's up?"

"I just don't know what to say to you."

"How can you not know what to say to me? What are you talking about?"

"I just feel awkward. This is uncomfortable. . . ."

"Why, 'cause you ripped my guts out? You feel uncomfortable about that?"

"Will . . ."

"Oh, I know you didn't mean to. I know you're sorry."

"Do we have to do this?"

I just wanted him to leave.

"Do what? Talk about our feelings? Don't tell me, now that I'm finally opening up, you don't want to hear it. Well, isn't that rich."

I just sat next to him on the sofa, dressed in my house sweatpants and loose T-shirt, face scrubbed of makeup, hair in a ponytail, staring at the floor.

"You look beautiful."

He reached out to touch my face and I moved away.

He got up and pulled me by my hands to stand.

"I'm going to go. I don't want to make you uncomfortable."

I felt relieved and let him hug me.

"Just tell me this: If it weren't for Miles would you give this another go?"

"I don't know, Will. I honestly don't know."

He looked down into my eyes, his hair a little shaggy like I liked it.

"You know I don't give up easily?"

I nodded my head, knowing the truth, wishing it were different.

"I know."

When he left, I began to breathe, realizing I hadn't the whole time he was here.

The next day I got up and went to the deli and bought bagels like a dutiful daughter and waited to hear from Mom, who would be delivering Abby here. When the buzzer rang I stood at my door, where I could see them get off the elevator. Behind Mom was a thin, long-haired woman who looked like an extra from *A Mighty Wind*, complete with that same quasi-angelic, quasi-stoned comportment. She was dressed in jeans and a denim shirt and lots of silver and turquoise jewelry.

"Precious Aisha," she said as she walked toward me with her arms open. I couldn't even think about doing anything but returning her enthusiasm. We hugged each other long and hard and all the doubts I'd had about what I was feeling evaporated like dust. She kissed me on my cheek and whispered how wonderful it was to meet me.

Mom walked into the apartment, past us, probably to make sure I'd cleaned up.

We made small talk about her trip, New York, in my apartment for a while. I proudly offered them bagels only to learn she didn't eat white flour but she would take me up on a cup of tea.

"There's a nice organic restaurant in the neighborhood, we could walk there," I offered.

Mom made a face behind Abby's back but said that sounded perfect.

"Are you losing weight?" I said, noticing Mom for the first time today.

She nodded and smiled broadly.

"I am. I'm doing Weight Watchers and Abby's been sending me some great low-fat vegetarian recipes."

"You, a vegetarian?"

"She's discovered portobello mushrooms . . . she gets her meat fix," Abby tells me conspiratorially.

We walked to the restaurant, Abby and I arm in arm, and I couldn't help feeling overwhelmed by her warmth, her acceptance of me, a stranger. I thought of the contrast to what I'd gotten from Meredith, Will's mother, my almost mother-in-law who made me feel as if I might one day be treated as well as one of her Yorkies—all very politely, of course. She and Abby were probably the same age but that was about all they'd have in common.

"So, Camille tells me the marriage is off," Abby says over carob carrot cake.

"Yeah, it is."

"Are you okay with that?"

Mom interrupts by telling Abby that I'm already seeing someone else.

"That's my girl," Abby laughs. "No sense cryin' over yesterday's rain."

"So, who's the new boy?"

"His name is Miles and he's wonderful."

"Does he realize your worth?"

Damn, this one fits right into the Branch-family cabal. She goes right to the point, no dancing around words for her.

Mom laughed out loud.

It was a great question for which I didn't have an answer.

"I would hope so," I said.

"Well, you just need to make sure he does."

We closed the restaurant; they needed to set up for dinner so we moved on to the ubiquitous Starbucks. I'm sure Earth Mama Abby had never been in one, but she was cool, asked lots of questions about their product and was pleasantly surprised to learn that she could get herbal tea with soy milk.

I didn't know what to ask about my real father, where to begin.

"Aisha, I want you to know how sorry I am that you didn't know Adam. He really was a remarkable young man, if I may say so."

"You may say so," Mom piped in.

"Thank you, Camille. I know this is probably weird for you, Aisha, to be looking at this strange White woman who's your grandma and you've never laid eyes on before."

I took a sip and nodded but told her that it wasn't as odd as I'd thought it was going to be.

"Good, because I feel a kinship with your mother and I hope you'll allow me to become a part of your life. Whatever you want to offer, I'll take."

I looked at Mom, who wiped a tear away, and we smiled at each other.

"Abby, you are a dear and I think Aisha would agree with me that we're fortunate to have you come into our life," Mom said.

"You make an old woman's day," Abby said, not trying to hide her tears.

"You don't look old. How old are you?" I said, needing to lighten the moment.

"I'm sixty-four next Monday."

"Ah, a Taurus. Good people," Mom said.

"Oh brother, here we go, she'll be doing your chart next, Ab . . . I don't know what to call you."

"Whatever you're comfortable with, babe: Abby, Grandma, Granny, Honey Baby."

We all laughed. She was a hoot.

"Did my dad have your sense of humor?"

She looked away, as if really trying to remember, trying to picture him.

"He did, when he was little, before his father died and he changed. I used to tell him he was going to be a comedian. . . ."

"I saw that too, but it wasn't ha-ha funny. He was rueful and very sarcastic," said Mom.

"Yeah, that's after he'd become angry."

We sat silent for a moment, each of us in her own head, with her own version of Adam. They, at least, had a visual talking human. I had nothing.

"I need to go," I said, abruptly.

"Oh, okay," Abby said.

"You have a hot date?" Mom asked.

"No, I don't have any plans, but I'm tired and you know I wanna write in my journal, plan my outfits for the week for my new job. . . ."

"Oh, yes, your mom told me, *French Vogue,* very, how you say, *très bien.*"

"*Oui, merci beaucoup,* madame. How about I call you *mon petit chou?*"

"Yes, *oui,*" her eyes lit up, "*mon petit chou.*"

We got up from our chairs.

"We'll walk you back. My car's in the lot near your building."

When we got to my building and hugs were made, Abby asked if it would be okay if she sent me pictures and little things about Adam.

"Yes, I'd like that."

"It's done. Thank you, my dear." She hugged me again.

"Now, we're going back to the 'burbs, I'm taking her to meet Grandma."

"Oh, good luck."

We laughed; Abby looked confused and waved good-bye.

It was Saturday night and I had no plans; hadn't heard from Miles in a few days and didn't want to have the feeling of anxiety that was rumbling around in the pit of my stomach.

So I hadn't heard from him. He's busy. Doesn't necessarily mean he's with another woman. Who am I kidding?

Cedra called and said Will had been calling her, bending her ear about how much he missed me, how fucked up things were, how much better he'd be if I'd give him another chance, asking, *Does she talk about me?*

"It's pathetic. Please do something about that boy."

"Like what? I've broken off with him, there's nothing else I can do."

"Well, he's under the impression that there's hope of some kind of reconciliation. Maybe you should be firmer with him."

"Cedra, believe me, there's nothing else I can do. He's just not used to not getting what he wants."

"Well, that's obvious, but I know how you like to be adored. You sure you haven't given him a little hope?"

It was another one of her mean comments that stung and not for its trueness; it made me question how long I could consider her my best friend.

"I'm sure."

I suddenly remember the time I overheard some Jack and

Jill girls talking about me. Cedra was in the room—the finished basement of somebody's house during a mother's meeting upstairs. A few of the girls were going on about me, *Aisha did this, she wore that,* I can't remember what they'd said about me now because it was then, as it is now, unimportant to me. I just know it was one of those who-does-she-think-she-is sessions that Grandma and my mom had warned me about for they too had been subjected to such in their younger years. I just figured it was a Branch family ritual. But the fact that Cedra, my dear friend, didn't come to my defense stayed with me. She didn't jump in and join them, but she didn't say anything either. I never said anything to her about it and I hadn't really thought about it—until now. I knew that she didn't dislike me like the other girls. I didn't think that was possible, but could it be that she was jealous of me? How could that be? She was the brain who won all kinds of awards and competitions; she was the one everybody wanted to be friends with in Jack and Jill, in whose house every party was held. Her mother was the fashionable one who knew where to get the best prices on designer clothes and would freely take all of us shopping with her. Yeah, her mom got dogged by her dad, but everybody has something bad to go through. It was really embarrassing when her dad ran off with her mother's sorority sister, but Cedra and her mom seemed to bounce back from them, well, in a way. Her mother does still drink a little too much.

"Are you okay? You sound funny?"

*Duh,* I wanted to say, but resisted. I just wasn't up to having another big confrontation with her.

"No, I'm alright," I lied, tasting the bile of betrayal. "I met my new grandma today," changing the subject.

"Oh yeah, how was that?"

"Weird. Here's this White woman, this stranger, who looks

like the poster child from the sixties, who's like all lovin' me . . ."

"Yeah, that would freak me out."

"I mean, I don't know her."

"Yeah."

"And I never really thought much about my dad being mixed, I mean I didn't even know about him until I was damn near grown and by then it really didn't mean anything."

"I know. . . ."

"I guess if I'd grown up seeing him all the time, knowing he was half, I might feel different, but I just feel Black."

"You are Black."

"Yeah."

"Look, Ash, we all mixed at some point in this fucking great land of ours. Everybody was fucking us in the dark and busy tryin' to pretend they wasn't but all you have to do is look at us. Most of us don't look straight-up African, so don't go tripping about it, 'cause just about everybody is. . . ."

"Yeah, you're right."

"Are you sure you're okay? You want me to come over?"

That was the last thing I wanted. I just wanted to get off the phone with her and not speak with her for a while. I knew I couldn't really put my feelings into words that she would understand, at least not now. Friends are supposed to help us fill in those blanks. I told Cedra I was tired and she let me get off the phone. There is comfort in old friends, but sometimes I wonder if Cedra and I hadn't grown up together, if we'd be friends as adults. She can be so intolerant, so cynical, so damn sure.

Against my better judgment, I called Miles. He was out somewhere, I'd called him on his cell, and he told me he was having drinks. I didn't dare ask with whom, but knew it was a woman, a date, maybe even that Lisa Ondosdi, the anchorwoman who called the other night, one of my competitors. I was feeling sorry for myself.

"So I met my dad's mom today," I told him, knowing this was not the time to have this conversation.

"Really? How'd it go?"

I could hear ice clinking, people talking, music in the background.

"It was good. She's cool."

"Good. I'd like to hear all about it."

"I know I know, you're busy. I'll talk to you later."

I hung up before he could say anything else. I felt like a stupid little girl.

I later found out that Miles had been having drinks with Natasha, who was in town on business, and was in fact talking to her about me.

He and I had brunch the next day.

"So you talked to her, your ex-fiancée, about me? Isn't that weird?"

Miles was digging into his egg-white frittata.

"Naw, she and I are friends and I trust her judgment."

"So, you were asking her for advice about me?"

Miles put his fork down and looked at me.

"No, but I was bouncing something off her. . . ."

"Which was?"

"Boy, you are like a dog with a bone, you're relentless."

I smiled my most charming smile at him.

"She knows me well and she could tell based on whatever, I guess the way I'd mentioned you in the past, that I really care about you."

"And . . ."

"And to be honest, I'm struggling with the age difference between us."

I looked at him, as if this were a nonissue for me.

"Are you looking for reasons not to be with me?"

He was eating again.

"Baby I think you know I'm not one to make up reasons. I'm a pretty straightforward guy. If I didn't want you, I'd tell you that."

"But—" I said, sipping a peach mimosa.

"I'm sixteen years older than you, that's a lot."

"Yeah, but I don't think it matters that much. If I'm willing . . ."

"Well, news flash, dearest, it's not just about you."

# CHAPTER 25

# Camille Puts Down Her Baggage

## *Camille*

I was losing weight, exercising and, as the kids say, smelling myself. I spent a lot of time talking with Abby, who was so encouraging and reminded me that I was still a vibrant woman. I had been acting her age, had hung up so much of my vital, sexual self and had become a fat, boring woman living in a box. I'd become everything I railed against. Abby had become a close friend, again forcing me to realize that I hadn't had any. My peers were long gone, once I became a teenage single mother. The only ones left were the victims—the ones who blamed everything wrong in their lives on someone or something else; saw the Man's handiwork behind everything bad. I'd been sucked in by these people, made to think they were my people, but Geneva, knowing different, would gladly point out that we had as much in common as "a pig and a tutu." But there had been a common thread: resentment. I was bitter for having had to give up being young and free, for being too proud to take money from my parents, for working like a field slave and going without nice things that I was used to having—all to have the righteous anger of doing it on my own. I'd been carrying around a fleet of luggage filled with my indignities but now, like the pounds, I was letting it go.

Abby and I pulled up to Geneva's house and saw her at the window, no doubt mad 'cause we took longer than I had promised. Mabel, the lady who helped her look after the house, had already left, but had made enough food for a medieval feast.

Mama opened the door and greeted us:

"What the hell took you so long?"

"Abby, this is Geneva; Geneva, meet Abby."

Most people would be a little embarrassed to be caught carrying on in front of a total stranger. Not Geneva.

"Nice to meet you, Abby, come on in."

Abby was immediately drawn to a wall of photographs that ran from the foyer wall into my parents' living room. There were pictures of Dad with Dizzy, Miles, Monk, Duke Ellington, Louis Armstrong, Sarah Vaughan, Billie, Charlie Parker, Coltrane and, of course, with Carmen McRae. In each picture Daddy wore the same, what he used to call, thirty-two grin. "That's when you try to show all your teeth."

"Oh, here's Carmen McRae. I loved her," Abby said.

"So did my dad."

"He wanted to name you Carmen," Mom said. Her voice trailed off, but I heard her say "over my dead body." "We compromised on the name Camille."

I'd always sensed a little tension around Dad's affection for Carmen but until now didn't realize that it was more than a professional relationship. Of course, getting Mom to talk about this was not going to happen.

"My God, I had no idea your dad was this big."

We joined her in the living room, where I beamed; I loved showing Daddy off. Mom looked warily at Abby.

"Yeah, he was big time," I said.

"Not as big as he should've been," Geneva added.

"Come on in the kitchen. Mabel made enough food to feed Biafra."

Abby looked at me and smiled warmly, as if to say, *Now I understand.*

"So, how's my girl?" Geneva said, standing over the table as we put small amounts of food on her good yellow-and-white plates.

"She's fine. You know she has a new job?"

"Yeah, she called me the other night. She sounds excited."

"Yes, she'll be great," Abby said.

"Well, of course she will, Branch women succeed at whatever we try," Geneva said, snappishly.

Okay, so this wasn't going so well.

"Well, I didn't mean . . ."

"I know, you don't know what you meant. You don't know her."

"Well, I . . ."

I put my hand over Abby's to stop her from remaining on this leaking ship.

"These greens are delicious, Geneva, did you make them?" Abby, a quick study, said.

"Naw, I don't cook," she said proudly, a lie I'd never heard her tell and with such pride.

"My . . ." I looked at her, waiting for her to say the word although I knew she wouldn't be able to bring herself to say, *My girl.* "The lady who helps me around the house made them."

"I see," Abby said.

I looked at my mother, but she wouldn't meet my gaze.

"So," Geneva said, sitting down at the head of the kitchen table. "I was sorry to hear about your son."

Abby looked up from her plate and silently acknowledged the condolence.

"I'd never met him," Geneva said.

"Yes, you did," I said.

"Yes, but I didn't know he was your boyfriend. You kept that from us."

"Did you meet Camille before?" Geneva asked.

Abby looked at her, surprised this time, and said no.

"But I didn't meet any of Adam's friends during that time. He closed himself off from me, didn't really want to have me in his life."

"Why not?" Geneva said, sounding like a prosecutor.

"He was angry at me, probably at the world. His father had died. . . ."

"Yeah, Camille told me all this, but I have to tell you, Abby, I'm feeling like there was something missing, maybe something you're not telling or that you didn't know."

Boy, at seventy-two you really do say exactly what you want to say.

Abby sat up straight and put down her fork. She looked directly at Geneva.

"My son is dead. My husband is dead and I don't have anything to hide," Abby said, and she picked up her fork and continued to eat her greens.

"Probably not, but there was probably something about the boy you, not being Black, that you just didn't understand."

Abby looked wounded.

"Mom," I said, calling her off, realizing she knew exactly what she was doing, even using the word *Black,* which she hardly ever "remembered" to say, preferring *colored* instead. "That's enough."

I wanted to protect Abby.

"No, it's okay. I want to hear what Geneva has to say," Abby said.

She didn't need my protection.

"Well, I think the anger was probably just at realizing he was Black; even though his mama was White, he still got treated like a . . . And you could never understand what that felt like."

Geneva sat back in her seat as if to say, *I've spoken my piece now.*

"You know, Adam's father and I tried to raise him to see people, to see beyond color and religion and things that don't make a person who he is, and when he was little, we were able to do that, but . . ."

"They grow up and we can't protect them. I know," Geneva said, reaching out to pat Abby's hand.

I felt my stomach feel less tight.

We spent the rest of the day with Geneva, who, it turns out, told Abby all about our trip to Connecticut and our visit with Trudy.

"She's not doing well," Geneva said to no one in particular.

My mother was no longer trying to hide her grief, she was wearing her sadness now.

# CHAPTER 26

# A Blurred Identity

## *Aisha*

Springtime in Paris is time for the fall shows and true to her word, Martine had me come over and even got me into the coveted fashion shows. Paris is a complete mad scene during this time, the streets are packed with traffic, the big editors have limos and Martine let me ride with her, knowing that I wasn't up to dealing with the traffic challenges, but I couldn't sit in the front rows with her, those seats were strictly reserved for the top editors-in-chief and fashion editors and, these days, celebrities—and big ones like Nicole Kidman and Madonna. The designers held their shows in unusual places, like school gymnasiums or old firehouses. There was no one central fashion location and there were as many as twelve shows a day. I was going from eight in the morning till midnight every day for a week. I was exhilarated and exhausted at the same time. I was stuck with the woman who would be my direct boss, head stylist, Johanna Wyeth—piece of work. She was an American, a

Francophile, an Upper East Side girl like the ones Will grew up with who really didn't have any interest in teaching me the ropes.

Even with designers going into high competition with each other to become more outrageous than the next, the real show was outside—the paparazzi jockeying for the best candid on-the-street shot of fashion folk and the fashion folk jockeying to be photographed, quoted and generally stabbing each other in the back. There was madness trying to get into the shows, even though I had the proper-color ticket. Mobs of people were constantly trying to maneuver in without one; the ticket colors changed every day to try to keep the uninvited from scamming a way in. Most of the time, I didn't even have a seat; my ticket gave me entrée, but I had to stand in the back. The signature look to drape one's stick-thin body was high-skinny heeled sandals, skirts to the knee and some kind of Chanelish jacket and bare legs. Even during the fall—no matter how cold—bare legs were the only way. On my last day, Lagerfeld had his show at the Louvre, where only the biggest names show. I was actually seated, although I couldn't see much of the stage; I sat watching the busy and fabulous and waited for the show to start. The presenters were waiting for the editor of American *Vogue*, who was caught in traffic, to show up before they started. They'll hold the shows for the big editors. I sat between the flaxen-haired Johanna and another girl with der-matological-perfected skin, who talked to each other over me, as if I weren't there. I didn't know a soul other than Martine, who, in this crowd, became more caricature than a real person. I wished I had somebody to share this with, to talk about these people with, but I was in this world all alone and I didn't think I'd be capable of ever re-creating it in the retelling. I found myself wishing for a pajama night with Grandma.

After dragging myself back to my hotel, I walked into the small, artfully decorated lobby and there was someone who looked familiar sitting in an armchair, but I thought, No, can't be, it's just some Parisian who looks like Will. I looked closer and he looked up from his magazine. He got up and walked toward me.

"What the hell?"

"I know, what am I doing here? It's crazy, but I thought, I've gotta see her. You've gotta know how much I miss you and I want you back."

"Will, I can't . . . I'm so tired right now."

"Come on, let me walk you to your room."

I had no resistance and was happy to have someone be nice to me. He took my key from my hand and led me to the elevator.

Inside, I leaned my poor, tired body against the wall of the tiny lift.

I looked at him and recognized the person I'd fallen for.

"When did you get here?"

"Oh, a few hours ago."

"How'd you find me?"

"Cedra told me where you were staying."

We walked down the short hall to my door.

"I don't think you should come in," I said, standing in front of the door.

"That's fine. I have a place to stay. I just needed to see you and . . ."

He leaned over and placed his lips on my forehead. I didn't resist.

"I have to get up so early. Tomorrow's the last day, thank God."

"Fine. I'll meet you for drinks, how about nine?"

"Will, I don't know. . . ."

"Okay, you don't have to commit now. I'll call you tomorrow evening. If you're up to it, fine. If not, I'll see you back in New York. Okay?"

I was so glad that he didn't try to push himself on me.

"Fine, that sounds fine."

With that I turned and rolled onto the other side of the door.

"*A toute à l'heure*," he said as I locked the door.

"*A toute à l'heure*," I uttered back.

I stepped out of my pants and took off my jacket and got into bed. I was asleep before the room got dark.

When the wake up call came the next morning, I wasn't sure if I'd actually seen Will or if I'd dreamed it. It wasn't until I'd had my coffee and chocolate croissant that I was sure he had actually been here.

On the way in the car, Martine, who was used to this circus, seemed open and relaxed.

"Did you sleep well?"

"I did, but the weirdest thing happened."

She looked at me and raised her perfectly arched eyebrow.

"My ex-fiancé showed up at my hotel."

"From America?"

"Yes."

"Oui, intrigue. How ex is he?"

"It's been a few months."

"Is he brokenhearted?"

"I guess so, more than I realized."

"Is he the one you were lunching with when I saw you at Tocqueville?"

"Oh no, that's the current one."

Martine raised her brow, again.

"So why did you break off with him?"

"I fell passionately in love with someone else—the one you saw me with."

"Mmm. So there was a manqué of passion with the fiancé?"

"Yes, and I think a basic incompatibility."

"Ah, oui, you Americans and your compatibility, men and women are all incompatible. It is our nature."

"Yes, but . . ."

"What is he like, the ex?"

"He's rich, he's remote, he's—"

"He is trust-fund rich or self-made rich?"

"Trust fund."

"Ah, I see, and this other? He is self-made, yes?'

"Yes."

"Ah, I remember him, *très séduisant,* how you say, seductive. They are so much more when they are hungry. It is true."

It is true. I realize I'd been way too busy to think much of Miles since I'd been away. It was true. He was delightfully omnivorous and it was sexy, but he was more. I looked out the window at the throngs of people on foot and wanted nothing more than to be back in New York, with Miles. I said a prayer that he missed me too.

"So what are you going to do about this fiancé? Will you send him packing?"

"I think I have to."

"But to waste your trip to Paris and not have a tryst? Who would know?"

She was right about trysting in Paris. Not to seemed wasteful. Sex was in the ozone here.

The city made me want to show cleavage and smoke cigarettes and neck in public, but did I want to do any of that with Will?

"I've been so busy since I've been here that I haven't even returned Miles's calls."

"*Bon*, he'll be dying for you when you return."

The shows came and went in the usual blur of fabulosity, but at the end instead of being dog tired as I'd anticipated, I was energized, perhaps because I'd completed something of a hazing, as Martine had said I would.

"Now we go for dinner, have some champagne. Won't you come?"

Johanna, a French gay male editor and I were with Martine. I didn't really want to, all that smoking and speaking French and trying to keep up would surely give me a headache, but I also didn't want to say no to my boss.

Johanna glared at me.

"How about I just come for drinks. I really need to get back to my room," I said, giving her the evil eye back.

"Of course, have some champagne and go. It's fine," Martine said.

So, that's what we did. After two glasses of the best champagne I'd ever tasted, I felt like I could do anything, even make Johanna want to be my friend. I said au revoir to everyone, thanking them all for sharing their talents with me—although I'm not sure how exactly they were talented—and headed back to my hotel. I wanted to call Miles, but it was four in the morning in New York. I could wait three hours and then call.

So I called Will instead.

"I've been waiting for you to call. You feel like eating?"

I sighed, he sounded so eager.

"Come on, Ash, just dinner. We're in Paris. I'm at this great place. Where are you?"

"I'm at my hotel."

"I'm a few blocks away. Oh come on, you can walk here."

In my mind I go through the lists of options: dinner alone in my room, somehow busy myself until I can call Miles, pack and try for an earlier flight home.

"As tempting as your offer is, Will, I'm going to pass. I need to pack and get home."

"To Miles?"

"You have a good time. . . ."

"Don't hang up—"

"I really need to go."

"I shouldn't have said that. I'm sorry. Just answer this, did you ever love me?"

"Of course I did."

"So what happened to it?"

"I don't know."

"Why don't you rest a little and I'll call you later."

"Okay, you do that."

After I packed my things, I was still too antsy to stay in my room. I decided to have something to eat downstairs at the bar.

I ordered some mussels in butter and wine—isn't everything in Paris—and I refused a nice wine. I was still buzzing from the champagne earlier.

As I ate, the restaurant got louder and more crowded. It was Friday night.

A man who looked like he might have been a Black American sat a few stools away from me and was chatting amiably in French with the bartender. While his French was fluent, I could tell that he wasn't quite a native speaker.

I looked at him and realized he could've been from east or South Africa; he could've been Sri Lankan or Haitian, almost anything. I decided it was a good thing to have a blurred identity. I said hello and he smiled and said it back.

"You here on business?" I asked.

He nodded and said sort of.

"You mind if I join you?"

"Not at all."

I wanted some kind of company.

He scooted down two stools.

He looked about fifty, was short with a mixed gray beard and a neatly trimmed head full of hair.

"I'm Richard Paul Brown," he said, sticking out his hand.

"I'm Aisha Branch McCovney."

"Nice to meet you, Aisha. So what brings a pretty little Black American girl like you to Paris?"

I told him my work story.

"Ah, so what'd you think of the shows?"

"Don't tell me you're in the business."

He was wearing a black shirt and tweed blazer with patches on the elbows.

"Oh, no, no, I'm a photographer. I work for a wire service. I'm here for totally other reasons."

"Yeah, I was going to say . . ."

"What, my clothes don't look couture?"

I laughingly told him they didn't.

"I think I might be insulted."

"Don't be; after the crap I've seen this week, you could take it as a compliment."

"Take bad?"

"Well, let's just say I was underwhelmed for my first experience."

"So where in the States do you live?"

"How'd you know that I was a Black American? I was thinking you could be almost anything."

"It was your dress and body language."

"I couldn't pass for French?"

"You were too friendly."

"I live in New York, what about you? Where do you live?"

"I live in Philly, grew up there, but I've lived all over, around the world for the past twenty years."

"Really? Where've you lived?"

"Well, I spent seven years in Africa, in Ghana, Ethiopia, Somalia, Kenya, South Africa. Then I was in Asia—Vietnam, Korea, and Thailand. . . ."

"Wow. Was it great?"

"It was, for a while, then it wasn't. I started really missing home."

"So do you have a family?"

"Nope. I had a wife, a Kenyan, who divorced me. We have a son who's grown now. What about you? You married?"

"No, I just broke it off, almost married; and I'm seeing someone now. I'm in love. Can I ask you how old you are?"

"How old do you think?" He turned to the side, tilting up his profile.

"I don't know, forty-five?"

"Bless you, my child. I'm fifty-three."

We exchanged cards, had a glass of wine together.

"So do people call you Richard or Paul?"

"My friends call me Richard Paul."

"So are you seeing anyone?"

"I'm not seeing anyone special at the moment. Why?"

"I'd like you to meet my mom."

He laughed out loud.

"Your mom? How old is she?"

"She's forty-five."

"And where's your dad?"

"They're divorced."

"I see. Well, was it a good divorce? Or is your mom all evil and hates men?"

"I guess you could say it was good, although I think that's a weird word to describe divorce."

"Yeah, it is, but you get the point."

"She doesn't hate men."

"Do you look like your mother?"

"She's attractive, but no, we don't look that much alike."

"You have a picture?"

"I don't, but does it matter that much?"

"No, no. I was just curious, that's all."

"Why don't you give me your e-mail address. . . ."

When I got back to my room, I called Miles. I still had a few hours before I had to catch my flight home.

"Hey, baby," he said, sounding groggy.

"Did I wake you up?"

"Yeah, but that's okay. How're you? How's Paris?"

"Great. I'm good, tired—but good."

"Busy, huh?"

"Oh man, more than I could ever imagine, but I've learned so much. Martine's really been great."

"Good, Ish, I'm glad to hear it. So when are you coming home? I miss you."

It was the first time he'd initiated something like this and I felt all weak and excited in my stomach.

"I'll be in today. My flight leaves at noon so I'll be there about one."

"Today!" He was uncharacteristically excited.

"Yeah, today."

"What airline? Maybe I'll meet you at the airport."

"You will?"

"I'm heading out. I've got to go to Frankfurt for this deal."

"Oh," I said, a little disappointed that he wouldn't be coming just to see me.

"I'm on Air France, my flight is due to land at one-twenty."

"Okay, I'll be at your gate."

We hung up and I couldn't tell how I was feeling. I couldn't wait to see him, but I also felt like I needed to turn it down a little.

I went into the tiny bathroom and looked in the mirror and realized I looked a mess, hadn't washed my hair since I'd been in Paris. There was no time and I'd been wearing it up and curly and now all the products I've been using needed to be washed out. I ran a bath, put in some of the free ginger-scented bath products and let the water cover me.

I lathered myself and loved the feel of my breasts and my inner thighs. I was getting myself worked up and remembered I needed to wash my hair; scrubbing myself just turned me on even more; after practically falling asleep in the tub, I climbed out and wrapped myself in the hotel robe.

I found my cell and called Will.

"I'm getting ready to leave, but you could come over for a quick coffee."

"I'm on my way."

All my clothes were packed, dirty, except for the jeans and black jacket I had on over my vintage bustier.

Will showed up ten minutes later.

"What were you, in the lobby?" I asked, letting him in.

"Practically; I'm staying a few blocks away."

He looked around the tiny room and then walked to the window, out to the tiny balcony.

"Nice view," he lied.

"Yeah, right. You want something? I ordered some crepes."

"Yeah, I'll have one. So, you heading back now?"

"In a little while."

"I'm glad you called. I have something I want to tell you."

We sat and ate at the little round table, sitting next to each other on the settee.

"I love your hair like that."

"Will, it's a mess."

"No, it's great. You're great."

He put down his cup and removed mine from my hand, looking me in the eyes all the while. He leaned in to me, kissing me hard while putting one hand into my bustier and the other unzipping my jeans. I pulled his lower hand away.

"Just let me make you . . ."

And I let him.

We sat slumped on the settee, with me spent and him looking at me. He was always unselfish in bed.

"I gotta get to the airport. What did you want to tell me?"

"Huh?"

"You said that there was something you wanted to tell me."

"Oh, yeah . . ."

I zipped myself up and walked to the hall table to look in the mirror.

"I came here 'cause I wanted to tell you something."

I turned from the mirror and looked at him.

"I'm not taking the art director job."

"Oh, why not? I thought you were into it?"

"Nah, I don't want it. I'm going to India for a while, go down to Sydney. I need to travel around, clear my head."

"Is this because of me?"

I looked at him, pleadingly, hoping it wasn't.

"No, it's what I want to do. Figure out some stuff, what I really want to do with my life."

"You might as well, take advantage . . ." I stopped myself, remembering you never talk to a rich person about money. I wanted to say, *Take advantage of all your possibilities, act like a real son of wealth,* but I resisted.

"Well, I think that sounds great. Will you spend time with your sister in India?"

"Hopefully. Emma and I used to be close, I'd like to get to know her again."

I walked over to him and kissed him on the forehead.

"I'm happy for you, Will."

"Ash, that's not all."

"Should I sit back down?"

"That day you came over and I was with Amanda?"

"Yeah," I said, picturing the two of them looking guilty in the foyer of his apartment.

"Well, she had spent the night and we did. . . ."

I looked at him, trying to understand the point of his telling me this now, deciding I didn't need to know why.

"Well, thanks for telling me that."

We rode downstairs in the elevator, not talking, but I was feeling fine about him, no anger, nothing. He kissed me on the cheek as I got into the taxi in front of the hotel.

"Can I call you when I'm back in New York?" he said.

He saw the hesitation in my eyes.

"I mean, as a friend."

"Of course, I want to hear about India."


I couldn't sleep on the flight because I was so anxious to see Miles and felt weird about what had happened with Will. Every time I tried to doze off, I'd wake up to seeing us making out like teenagers. The espresso at breakfast didn't help. I sat next to a woman traveling with her husband and little daughter; thankfully this flight wasn't swarming with fashionistas. I'd had enough of them. As much as I lived and breathed fashion, I wasn't like those women and I couldn't quite figure out what the difference was. Cynical Cedra would say, *It's because you have a brain in your head.* But I don't think they can be dismissed that easily. There are plenty of smart women in fashion; it's not the level of intelligence, I guess, as much as a difference in priorities. Some of these women would sell their babies for the latest, hottest new designer purse, where if I don't really like a thing, I don't care how hot it's supposed to be. It's a Branch earthiness, I guess, that prevents me from being too taken in by some of these fads.

I thought my heart would beat right out of my chest when the pilot announced our descent, but it still meant at least a half hour on the plane. They should wait till we're like five minutes away to make the announcement.

I got up to go to the bathroom, having to climb over the zonked-out mother whose three-year-old finally, halfway through the flight, stopped whining and fell asleep. Why do people give the mother the evil eye when the child acts crazy, like she's somehow willing the kid to do so? We should be giving her vodka tonics instead of steely glares.

I pulled my hair up, to see which way it looked better, deciding to leave it down, frizzy and curly. I splashed my face with cold water. I searched my cosmetics bag through my many freebies for a bronzer and a natural-looking lip gloss, added a little pink to my lips to brighten up this tired face; a quick sniff under the pits and dabbed a little Jo Malone on my wrists and in my little cleavage.


He was there. I could see him at the end of the long walkway, beaming at me. Thank God he didn't show up with flowers. I hate such clichéd displays. His being there was more than enough. I resisted running to him because I'm way too self-conscious, but I wanted to. I walked to him, let go of my bags and wrapped my arms around his neck; he wrapped his around my waist and we must have kissed for five minutes, 'cause I heard people grumbling as they stepped around us.

"Let me look at you," he said, holding my face in his hands.

"I think I look the same."

"Better. Hard work suits you."

"You think?"

"You hungry?"

"I could eat."

"I have over an hour. We could grab something here?"

We held hands through the gate. We found a little café and ordered french fries and fried clams, feeding each other.

"So, when are you coming back?"

"Oh, this is just a quick trip. I'll be back in two days."

Two days, I think, seems like an eternity.

"I didn't realize you were still doing a lot of the finance stuff."

"Sure. I just control my time more, but it can still get pretty intense."

"But you love it."

"I have to say, I do, even though the travel, especially internationally, is getting to me a lot more than it used to. I used to make three foreign trips a week, no problem, and I can't do that anymore."

"Slowing down in your old age?"

I ran my foot up his leg of his suit pants and the waitress came over, flirtatiously asking Miles if he wanted anything else.

This was so common, it was almost laughable. All kinds of women, young, old and middle-aged; professional and non;

Black, White, Asian, Latino, they all got a whiff of Miles's magic and wanted a piece.

"I'll have a piece of cheesecake," I said, letting her know she'd been ignoring me.

"And bring two forks," Miles added, smiling at me, knowing what I'd just done.

"Ish, you're somethin' else."

"Thank you."

# CHAPTER 27

# Make Me a Match

## *Camille*

I met Richard Paul Brown for dinner at a lovely wood-paneled jazz club/restaurant in the heart of downtown Philadelphia one Friday night. I took the train from work and got there in an hour and a half. We'd e-mailed each other our photographs so this wasn't a complete blind date. He was stockier than he appeared in his. I hoped he didn't think the same about me. I'd lost twenty pounds since my picture had been taken and I'd also cut my hair. My locks were gone and I now wore a very close-cropped natural style. My gray was white just at the temples and Aisha said I looked fly; Abby said the look was happening. Geneva called it elegant. Most important, I felt like a million bucks. It was amazing what sticking to something can do to one's sense of self. It's what I'd been preaching and now I was actually following my own advice.

I walked in and before my eyes could adjust to the darkness of the club, Richard Paul walked up to me.

"Camille?"

I smiled and looked at him.

"I'm impressed," I said.

"Well, thank you."

"No, I mean that you recognized me."

He laughed.

"Oh, my bad. I feel stupid."

"No, no, I'm impressed by you too."

He looked at me with gratitude and held out his arm.

"Shall we?"

We had a corner banquette.

"Nice place," I said, nervously adjusting the silverware.

"Yeah, it is. Two young brothers own it."

"Really?" I said, looking around.

"So, how was your trip down?"

"Fine. Fast."

"Good, good. Yeah, that Acela is really something."

"Mmm-hum."

I wondered how long we'd have to do small talk. I was really bad at it.

"So, you recognized me with my haircut?"

"Yes. Well, I'm a photographer, so I see beyond the mundane."

"Mmm."

"It looks nice. Very becoming."

"Thank you. I felt like it was time for a change."

"So, Camille, you're a social worker?"

"That's right."

"You do psychotherapy?"

"I do. You need some?" I laughed.

He laughed too. That was a good sign.

"Not right at this moment, but I've had some."

That's a good thing, I hope.

We ordered our dinners and a bottle of nice white wine.

After two glasses I was feeling that mellow welcome-to-the-weekend thing.

"So, you have a great kid, you know that?"

"Yes, my Aisha is a great girl."

"How's she doing?"

"Good. She's working hard. She's in love."

"Ah, the love of her life?"

"She told you about him, huh?"

"Yeah, she didn't use that term, but I kind of read between the lines."

"How's that?"

"Well, she'd recently ended her engagement and was seeing someone that was important enough for her to mention to me, so I figured there was probably some overlap."

"That's very astute, Richard Paul."

"So she met the new dude when she was engaged to the old dude?"

"Yeah, that's what happened."

"I think one of 'em showed up in Paris."

"Yeah, Will, her ex."

"Gotta give it to him, that was a power move."

I laughed at the notion.

"I guess it was. Too bad for him, it didn't change her mind. As a matter of fact, he wanted her to have dinner with him the night she met you. . . ."

"And now here we are. Seems like some kind of synchronicity."

"You think?"

I hadn't been on a date with someone I'd actually been interested in in so long that I didn't know what to do with myself. I was happy the wine was making me not care.

"So how come you haven't remarried?"

"I don't know. I was focused on raising Aisha, my career. I just didn't see the point."

"Yeah, I know what you mean. My career has been everything. It's why my wife finally left. She said she was sick of coming in second all the time."

"Can't blame her."

"Yeah, I don't, I just wish she hadn't taken my boy away. He's a grown man now and I don't know him."

"Well, you can't raise a child, moving all over like you were doing."

"Yeah, I guess."

"Life is all about choices, a lot of them tough ones, but you gotta make a decision and then stick by the ones you make. . . ."

I was rambling on but Richard Paul seemed to be hanging on my every word, as if I was spilling some valuable jewels and he was careful not to let any of them drop.

It was nice to be out with a man who had been places, seen things differently, different from America.

"So tell me about living in Africa."

"Big place; you wanna be more specific?"

"Um, Ghana?"

"Awesome. The people are among the kindest I've ever met. Um, it was great being there and looking like everybody else, for once in my life. That was everywhere in Africa, the blending in."

"Yeah, I'd really like that, I felt that way when I went to Spelman. I mean, it's not quite the same thing, but . . ."

"Yeah, it's a lot like that, where race becomes a nonissue. You realize how much space it takes up in your psyche here, when you go someplace where everybody looks like you."

"So why'd you come back?"

He took a swig of wine, finishing off his glass, and carefully put the glass back on the table.

"I missed home, but of course now that I'm back I'm wondering why."

I looked into this man's soulful eyes and liked the way it felt. I didn't know much about games and types to avoid since the last time I dated, cash machines were a novel invention. I liked what he said and how he said it and knew I wanted to get to know him better.

Just as we were unselfconsciously staring into each other's eyes, my cell phone rang. I'm not a cell phone user, but basically have one so my mother and Aisha can always reach me. Clients can leave a message on the service.

It was Mom and she was upset. Trudy had passed away. I told her I'd be on the next train home.

"Is everything alright?" he said, motioning for the check.

"That was my mother. Her best friend died today and she's very upset. . . ."

"Of course, let me get you to the train station."

Aunt Trudy and Mom had been friends since college. That was fifty-plus years. She was with Mom when she met Dad. They had been each other's constant support. Aunt Trudy kept an eye on MJ and me when we were in boarding school near her home in south Jersey, coming to get us for Sunday suppers and holidays when Dad had to perform somewhere and they couldn't come get us. Aunt Trudy was rock solid. When her husband retired, he had to drag her out to Arizona. She didn't want to be that far from VeVe, such a cute name for a woman I never experienced as cute; but Aunt Trudy did.

\* \* \*

I got home and found Mom vacuuming. It was what she did when she was truly at her end.

"Mom, it's almost midnight."

"I know what time it is, Camille, but this rug is just filthy. Mabel half cleans this house. . . ."

I put my hand on my mother's shoulder.

"Mom, put that down. Come sit."

She looked me in the eye and my heart broke for her. Her eyes were red and sadder than I could ever remember seeing.

"I'll get some sherry," I said, having her sit on the sofa.

I went into the liquor cabinet in the dining room and heard my mother mumbling something in the other room.

I brought out two glasses of sherry. We each quickly downed one.

"I just can't believe she's gone. Herbie said she was getting better, the doctor thought she might be able to travel and she had a heart attack, just like that. . . . Nobody even knew she had a bad heart. She was always so healthy, but they say that cancer . . ."

"Mom, I'm so sorry."

She looked at me as if she weren't sure where my voice was coming from.

"What am I gonna do without Trudy. You know we were planning our annual trip? We were going to go back to Vegas."

"I know, Mom."

"I'm all alone now. I'm really all alone."

There's some research that says losing a close friend can be more devastating even than losing a spouse. Aunt Trudy and Mom had been doing their annual trips together for twenty-five years, ever since their kids were grown and gone. They'd been to Rome, Prague, Barcelona and a cruise to Alaska and lately they'd been doing Las Vegas. Mom liked the shopping and Trudy loved to gamble. They bickered like two roosters, but they understood each other better than anyone else, including their husbands. I envied their friendship and assumed I'd have one like theirs someday. It set the bar high for me and Mom always used to say, *You're lucky if God gives you one good friend in this life.* She certainly had one in Trudy and she taught both Aisha and me that if you ever had to question a tone or a deed from a friend, she wasn't a friend. You just know that person means you well. I used to think my mother was just harsh or didn't want me to have any friends, but she was just trying to help me find what she had in Aunt Trudy.

# CHAPTER 28

## The Person the Lord Intended

## *Aisha*

I sat on the floor of Miles's apartment going over my list of potential investors one more time, figuring out exactly how much I was asking for, before calling Grandma. Since Aunt Trudy died, I called her every day. I still worked as an assistant freelance stylist at *French Vogue*—the new magazine Martine had talked about never did get off the ground, about which I was not disappointed. Martine, however, had recounted how sad she'd been that they couldn't get enough advertising support—*aucune vision,* she'd complained about the lack of vision she'd faced. The last time I saw her we had champagne at the Four Seasons after a shoot. I told her all about my new venture. I'd found my calling. I was designing dresses for African women who had fistulas—holes in the tissue between the vagina and the bladder or rectum that prevent them from controlling their urine and waste.

"How'd you know about such?"

"I saw it on Oprah. She featured this Australian doctor Dr. Hamlin who had opened a hospital in Addis Ababa, Ethiopia, and did free surgeries to repair these women—many of them young girls—I mean they get married at like twelve."

"*Mon Dieu.*"

"Their bodies aren't prepared to deliver a child and there are no drugs for the pain. They are just in labor. Here, if there's a problem getting the baby out, you just have a C-section. They don't do caesareans there, so the baby dies inside them and in pushing the baby out a hole develops inside the bladder. They can't control their urine or waste and the husbands reject them because of their smell. He sends the woman back to her parents, to her village, where they are further ostracized, again because of the smell. The parents build a separate hut on the family land, but away from the rest of the family. I couldn't get these girls out of my head, with the doctor saying without the surgery these beautiful, young girls are ruined with no hope of being cured. How could their lives be over before they were even twenty-one? I was driven to do more than just write a check."

"I would like to send a check," Martine said, reaching into her crocodile Anya Hindmarch handbag.


I had gotten the initial funding for the dresses from foundations and now I was writing proposals for private funding from wealthy people I'd met through Miles who like to invest in "green things," their term for good causes. For what I was once going to spend on a wedding dress, I could have paid for an entire village worth of surgeries. What *was* I thinking? I've designed cute, fitted T-shirts in gray with three pink *F*s on the front, which stand for Fashion Fights Fistulas, to bring more attention to this plight and to raise money for the hospital. I couldn't be happier doing something I love and knowing I'm helping these women. The doctor has invited me to come to Ethiopia for a visit and I even got a note from Oprah, which my grandmother has framed. It was a good thing that I was doing this now too because it gave Grandma something else to talk about, besides Aunt Trudy's death.

I called my grandmother and heard the TV blaring in the background. I wondered if her hearing was going.

"Grandma, did you know it cost less for fistula surgery than a Marc Jacobs pocketbook?"

I heard grandma laughing.

"Well, baby, I don't know what a Marc Jacobs pocketbook is, but I have to tell you I am so pleased you've found something that makes you so happy and that's so worthy."

"I know you are, Grandma, thank you, but an operation only cost four hundred fifty dollars, that's not even one Marc Jacobs purse," I said.

"Did I tell you that *mon petit*—" I stopped myself 'cause I knew Grandma hated that I had this nickname for Abby. She hated that I now had another grandmother.

"Did I tell you that Abby's food co-op sent a nice donation?"

"No you didn't, but that's very nice."

I could hear the strain in her voice and decided now was as good a time as any to tell her what I'd been meaning to.

"You do know, Grandma, nobody could come between us, don't you? I mean, what we have is so special."

"Aisha, I don't need for you to speak to me like I'm a child."

"I know that, Grandma, but I've been wanting to say this to you for a while. I know how you feel, but . . ."

"Little girl, you have no idea how I feel, okay? I appreciate what you're trying to say, but I'm fine about Abby. I actually think she's quite nice, for a White woman."

"Grandma!"

I heard her chuckling; I could just see her belly moving as she cracked herself up, as she did whenever she was being especially naughty.

"You know what I mean, child. I guess I do feel a little bit of what you're saying. . . . I have been the only grandma you've had your whole life and now all of a sudden there's this petite mon chu or whatever you call her and—"

"Grandma, why do you think I came up with something else to call her? You are the only grandma I've known, but that doesn't mean I can't let her into my heart—does it?"

"When did you get so grown?"

I knew this was her way of saying I was making a lot of sense.

"So when are we going to have a pajama night?"

I ran through my calendar in my head.

"How's tomorrow?"

"Really, you can come? Where's Miles?"

She sounded like I used to when Mom said she was volunteering at school.

"Yeah, I'll come and spend the night. Miles is away on business."

Miles had been away for a day and wouldn't be back for several more. I'd moved into his apartment a few months ago, after I started my business, after the one-year anniversary of his mother's death. He was my biggest supporter, talking up my plan to whoever would listen.

We turned a corner in our relationship when I'd insisted on going with him to Memphis to put flowers on her grave. He took me around his old neighborhood, introduced me to Mr.

Banks, who'd been his barber and a father figure from the time Miles was a toddler. He showed me his old elementary school and Christian Brothers Prep, where he'd gone to high school, and the field where he used to play baseball. I knew it would be difficult for him and I wanted to be there. It was a quick trip, only two days and a night, but it was the greatest window into who he is. We stayed at his mother's house, which remained exactly how it had been when she lived there. He wasn't prepared to sell it just yet, he'd said. On the plane ride back we sat next to each other, reading our respective magazines, in comfortable silence.

"Do you think your mom would've liked me?"

He put his copy of *The Economist* on his lap, took off his reading glasses and looked at me.

"Where'd that coming from?"

"I was just thinking that I would've loved to have known the woman who raised you. I think she did a wonderful job."

He nodded, sadly, looking as if he was trying to hold back tears. He looked away for a moment and then let me see him. He had tears in his eyes.

"She would have loved you, just like I do."

He put his hand over mine and I never felt so right.


I drove up to Grandma's in Miles's car and found her digging in her garden. It was time to plant the perennials again.

"Well, that's some kind of funny-lookin' car," she said, pushing herself up on a nearby bench.

"It's Miles's. It's a Mini Cooper. Isn't it cute?"

I kissed her on her cheek, which she normally just presents me with, but today she took off her gardening gloves and pulled me to her, hugging me tightly.

"I'm so glad you're here," she said, as if she hadn't seen me in ages.

"Grandma," I said, patting her back, "are you okay?"

She was crying. She led me to sit next to her on the white wrought-iron bench.

"Oh, baby, I've just been doing a lot of thinking lately, that's all." She took a tissue that was tucked in her shirtsleeve and blew her nose. "Damn allergies."

Yeah, right, I thought but had the good sense not to say.

"You wanna go inside? I brought a few of your favorite things," I said in a singsong voice.

She wiped her eyes with the back of her hand and fingered through the white bag I was carrying.

"I got you those chocolates you like and some cupcakes."

"The coconut ones?"

I nodded.

She licked her lips.

The last time I was here, I'd brought Miles to meet her. He introduced her to the coconut cupcakes from the Barefoot Contessa. I knew she had to have her own separate meeting with him, not through Mom or with her.

I don't know why I'd been nervous. I should've known that he'd charm the mess right out of her.

"Mrs. Branch," he took her hand between his and held it, "I'm Miles Browning. It's an absolute pleasure to make your acquaintance."

She looked at him, sized him up. I could read her mind: *I thought he'd be better-looking.* Which was some people's first reaction, but within seconds his attraction was undeniable. That Miles thing was so much bigger than conventional handsomeness.

Within minutes, she was eating him with a spoon. *Miles, can I get you more tea? Do you want another piece of cheese pie? Is there something else I can get for you?*

He regaled her with tales of growing up in Memphis. They were both native southerners and enjoyed that similarity, complaining about the coarseness of Yankees, the cruelness of some of their countrymen.

This time, as she often did, she had a pot on the stove.

"I thought we'd have some cabbage with our fish," she said, washing her hands in the kitchen sink.

I went to put my things down in Grandma's bedroom, which had remained the same since I was a little girl. I think she may have changed the bedcovers but they always remained similarly flowered and chintz.

I saw, at the foot of the bed, a photo album with old pictures and a magnifying glass. I opened the album and there were pictures of Uncle MJ—graduating from high school, in his basketball uniform at Princeton, where he played briefly. There was his Lawrenceville prom picture where Grandma or someone had taken something sharp and scratched out the person standing next to him, so that only Uncle MJ and a portion of blond shoulder-length hair could be seen.

There were pictures of Mom that I'd never seen: her, also in high school, with her uneven 'fro, standing in front of the Spelman College sign looking unsure of herself, but smiling.

Grandma called me from the kitchen and I went to join her. I set the table, trying to think of a way to bring up the pictures.

"So I was looking in your bedroom. . . ."

"Oh, I forgot to make the bread? Do you want corn bread?"

"No, that's alright, this is plenty and remember we have dessert."

"Right, right. So, you were saying?"

"Oh yeah, I saw you had pictures out. You working on something?"

"No. I was just putting them in the album, that's all."

I wondered why some weren't already in an album and asked her.

"Oh, I guess I never got around to putting them there."

"So who stabbed Uncle MJ's prom picture?"

We were sitting at the table now, about to bless the food.

"Can we say grace? I don't know about you, but I'm hungry," she said.

"Sure, sure."

She said grace, the one I know backward. "Gracious Lord, we're thankful for the food we're about to receive. Amen."

After a few forkfuls of cabbage Grandma confessed that she was the one who defaced the picture.

"I was so mad that he took that White gal to the prom, I couldn't see straight. There were Black girls there he could've asked."

"How many, Grandma, two or three?"

"That's enough. I'd even offered to bring Giselle, Trudy's gal, up to the school so he could meet her and maybe take her, but no, he had to take little Miss Goldilocks."

"So why'd you decide now to put the picture in the album?"

She looked at me.

"You know why? Because it just doesn't make any sense to hold on to all this foolishness, that's why. I spent too much time being angry at my children, time I could've spent just being with them, and now that I'm an old woman and I'm all alone, Major's gone and now Trudy I want to put all that away, all the things that kept them from wanting to be around me. I was thinking the other day, after I called MJ to tell him about

Trudy, that that was the first time I'd talked to him in I can't remember when he sounded genuinely happy to hear from me. We had a lovely conversation. He's coming for Trudy's funeral and I told him to bring his friend."

I couldn't believe what I was hearing. Grandma had refused to acknowledge that Uncle MJ had Bill, his "friend," much less to bring him to any family function. She wanted to pretend there was no Bill and even that my uncle wasn't gay. I guess miracles can happen.

"I think that's good, Grandma."

"I know, baby, even though I'm never gonna get over missing Trudy, I feel somehow like I'm just getting to be the person the Lord intended. Don't get me wrong though, I still don't like the fact that your uncle took that gal to the prom."

I looked at her and smiled knowing that I'd dodged her wrath during my engagement to Will. We finished up our dinner and I cleaned up the kitchen.

"Chile, if you knew what colored people went through when I was a girl, how hateful and mean those White folks were, you'd understand what I'm talking about."

"Well, you never told me any of those stories."

"Yeah, I know, because I didn't want to teach you about hate. What for? It'd just make you mean and hateful. I knew you'd learn what you was gonna learn on your own."

I sipped my sweet iced tea, the kind I can only get at Grandma's or down south.

"I'm going to finish the photo album and get into my pajamas," she said, getting up from the table.

"I'll put the dishes in the dishwasher and bring the treats upstairs. Do you think we need popcorn too?"

"I rented a movie, didn't I?"

"Okay, I'll make some popcorn."

Grandma had rented one of our favorites, *Splendor in the Grass*—so sad, so juicy. I've loved it since I was a little girl and hadn't seen it in a long time.

"That Natalie Wood was one pretty gal," Grandma said as the movie began, featuring the actress in her youth.

"So I know I'm probably not supposed to say this but . . ." Grandma said. "I'm so glad you and Will broke off."

Pause. Beat. I waited 'cause I know there was more coming.

"Will wasn't good enough for you, Aisha, and he never would've been able to appreciate you. He woulda been busy tryin' to make you feel grateful. It never would've worked out."

She dipped her hand into the popcorn bowl, which she'd held in her lap, turned her head back to the TV screen. Her piece said, *No reason for me to respond.*

"Pass the popcorn, Grandma."

# CHAPTER 29

# Wasn't Enough to Be a Deal Breaker

## *Camille*

I was pleased and surprised when I'd gotten the call from Cedra saying that she needed to talk. We used to talk all the time, but as often happens, once she grew up our conversations were less frequent. She'd learned to figure things out for herself, or to just keep things unresolved and locked inside, which is what too many people do. I met her at a restaurant in Manhattan. It used to stress me out to go to nice places in the city where I knew most of the people would be thin and nicely dressed, but now that I've lost forty pounds and still losing, I'm loving any chance I get to wear my new clothes. Cedra was seated at a back table already having a cocktail when I arrived. We hugged each other and I was pleased to see her looking so grown-up and prosperous, although she swears she's making serf's wages.

I ordered a diet soda and looked around, checking out familiar-looking faces of TV celebrities. The flowers, the attractive waiters and other patrons are far from how I usually spend my days.

"Well, this is nice," I said, looking at Cedra, more closely this time and realizing she didn't look that great.

She gained a little weight, her skin was broken out and her hair needed a trim.

"What's up, buttercup?" I said, trying to lighten the mood.

"I know you must think this is strange, calling out of the blue like this."

"No, not really, but you don't look good. What's on your mind?"

"So Aisha hasn't mentioned anything?"

"Like?"

"Well, we've been in a funky kind of place lately."

I did know, but I thought it best to let her tell her side of things.

"Why don't you tell me what's going on."

"Well, Ms. Mc, I don't know, I think I've hurt Aisha and you know how she is, she's just not really talking, but whenever I ask her about it she says everything is fine."

"Ask her about what?"

"Well, I've been a little rough with her and I'm afraid she's pulling away from me. She hasn't said anything to you?"

Our salads arrived and I was glad to have a moment to think about how much to reveal.

"She did mention a tiff you two had a while ago, when she was breaking up with Will."

"Yeah, I haven't really talked to her that much since, it's been like year. I mean we've gone through the motions over the phone, talk a couple times a month, but . . . and I know with starting the business and all that she's been super busy and I . . ."

"Well, you know in your gut that something's not right, right?"

"Yes, I feel her just moving away from me and you know what, I can't really blame her."

"Why do you say that?"

"I've haven't been the kind of friend I should be, that I used to be."

"So what happened?"

She was silent for a while, eating her salad, sipping her drink.

"I've been a jerk. I've been jealous of her and judgmental."

"Look, Cedra, you need stop being so hard on yourself. I know Aisha is a handful and it could be easy to be jealous of her, shoot, I've been jealous of her and she's my kid."

We both laughed.

She looked up at me from her plate as if a load had been lifted.

"Look, feelings of envy are normal. It's what we do about the feelings that counts. Aisha knows you love her. Why don't you make a date like you did with me and talk things out."

"Well, she's so busy now with Miles and the business and everything."

"I'm sure she'll make time for you."

Our entrées came. As I ate my half-portion grouper and vegetables, I felt as if I'd served my purpose for being here.

"You look great, by the way," Cedra said. "You've lost a lot of weight."

"I have, thank you, and you're a full-fledged architect now?"

"Yep, passed all my exams, completed my four years, eight if you count college, and I'm even doing a project solo."

"Really? What is it?"

"Well, it's just a pool house, but I'm really excited."

"Cedra, that's just great. I'm so proud of you. How's your mom?"

"Oh, she's fine, talking about moving to Florida, to Boca."

"Really? I'm surprised. She was always such a city person."

"Yeah, she claims there's more than just old people down there. I think she's tired of having to avoid my father and his new girlfriend every time she goes someplace."

"Yeah, I can understand that, the social circle being as tiny as it is."

"How's your mom? Aisha told me about Miss Trudy."

"Yes, the memorial service is coming up. Mom's okay, she's handling it."

"How's Mr. Lem doing?"

"Oh, Lem's fine, you know him. He'll work till they put him in the grave."

"Yeah, I read about his last case."

"Which one?"

"The police-brutality one?"

"Which one?" I said, laughing because so many of the cases at Lem's firm were against police using excessive violence.

"In Paterson."

"Oh yeah, that was a big one."

"Can I ask you a question?" Cedra said.

"Of course."

"Why'd you and Mr. Lem break up? You seemed so good together and even now, you seem fond of him and I know he's crazy about you and Aisha."

I thought about her question and other than the fact that I'd gotten bored with him, there really was no good reason. I didn't value money the way Lem did, but that, in retrospect, wasn't enough to be a deal breaker.

"I don't know, honey. At the time, I thought he was just

boring, but when I think about it now, he was a good husband. Aisha doesn't believe I do, but I make mistakes all the time."

I took a sip of Diet Pepsi.

"We all do."


I got home from my lunch with Cedra and resisted the temptation to get on the phone with Aisha. Let them work it out.

I stood in my front hall, sorting out the mail, picking out the large manila envelope from Abby. There were pictures of Adam as a baby; he was beautiful and naked in Abby's arms; in another black-and-white looking shyly into the camera in his dad's embrace. Adam's father looks like he spit Aisha out. I stare at the gray-and-oyster-colored pictures, with the serrated edges, fuzzy from age and antiquated technology, amazed that I'd never seen anyone who looked so much like her. In a color photograph, Adam looks about seven. I trace his hair, big loose curls. He had toffee skin, his mom's green eyes and mostly her nose, his dad's mouth and chin. There are many pictures of the three of them. They look like a happy family: Abby in her midriff and batik skirt, hippie hair parted down the middle; the dad with his bronze skin and heavy mustache and broad chest. They look like they loved each other. There was a note from Abby saying that these were for Aisha. "I promised her I'd send them, feel free to make copies for yourself, once I got them all together I realized I didn't have her new address. I love you, my dear. Abby."

I sat down on my sun porch, listening to the children traipse through the neighborhood, bottled-up energy released as they were let out of school. I thought about what a blessing Abby had been in my life. She was the mother-in-law of my dreams. She was even wearing down Mom's resistance to her.

Mom wanted to keep Abby at a distance, hoping that Aisha and I would too, but I told her that that wasn't going to happen. Abby was too wonderful to not have her in our lives, to which Mom said, "Of course she is, she's a White woman, she ain't got no reason not to be nice."

Abby sent Mom a basket of wildflowers and a lovely card when Trudy passed. Abby was the real thing and Mom was having a hard time rejecting her.

As happy as I was to have her in our lives, a part of me was so sad for what we'd all missed—the chance to have been a real family with Adam with us. I know one of the reasons Abby is clinging on so tight is her loss. How do you bury your child?

I put the pictures back inside the envelope to give to Aisha.

# CHAPTER 30

# No Surgery for Father Hunger

## *Aisha*

Miles came in from an overnight flight from France and looked beat. I was always glad to see him, though, no matter what condition he was in.

After I hugged and him and had him lie down on the sofa to give him a back rub, he noticed the pictures from Abby. Mom had sent them and I opened them and left them on the coffee table.

"What you got there?" he said, picking one up. "Who's this?" Miles said, pointing to my father's dad.

"He's my grandfather, my Dad's father."

"You look just like him and you look a lot like your dad too. Look at that."

"I know. Weird, huh?"

Miles looked at me, he could tell I'm about to lose it.

"Come here," he said, and pulling me to him. "Look at it this way, at least you have this much."

"I know, but I wish I had more, I just wish I could've known him, just seen him one time." I started to cry.

We sat together on the sofa holding each other, wishing our holes could be sewn up like the women in Africa, but there's no surgery for father hunger.

"Do you ever think about your father?"

"I used to, all the time."

"When you were little?"

"And when I was big. I wished that he'd show up at my graduation from high school and see all the awards I got, but he didn't. When I was graduating from college I told my mother not to invite him. I don't know if she did or not, but he didn't come. After that I kind of washed my hands of him."

"Did you really or did you just force yourself not to want him?"

Miles looked at me, amazed that I could zero in on what he'd done.

"How'd you get to be so wise?"

"Just the genes, I guess."

"He did get in touch with me after I finished business school. My name was in the papers for some deal and he sent me a card, told me he had diabetes and some other stuff, basically that he was dying. I guess he wanted me to come to Detroit but he didn't just come out and ask and I didn't go."

"Do you regret it?"

"I don't know. I'd like to think I don't, but who knows. You never know how this stuff plays itself out in your life. I know it has, I mean it's probably why I'm still single at damn near forty-five years old."

Herbie and Aunt Trudy's daughter Giselle decided to have the service at Aunt Trudy's home church, St. James, A.M.E. in

Newark. Even though Trudy and her husband had lived in South Jersey and Arizona for years, they maintained their membership at St. James and were considered part of the church family. It was only appropriate for her to be laid down there. Whenever Trudy visited Herbie and his family in Connecticut, she insisted that they drive all the way from Stamford to Newark to attend services at St. James.

Grandma hosted the repast and the house was filled with people from Trudy's and her life: classmates from Hampton Institute, some who lived in the area and some who traveled by car or train to pay their respects; there were many church members from Grandma's Presbyterian church; Uncle MJ came from San Francisco with his lover Bill; Abby came up from D.C. and even Mom's new friend Richard Paul came up from Philly; Dad was there looking uncomfortable with one of his "lady friends"; Miles came with me. Cedra even showed up.

I was prepared to see Grandma all cried out, but she was in a surprisingly upbeat mood, being the gracious host, telling funny stories about herself and Trudy, pointing out various pictures of the two of them from the collages she and I had made together and mounted on cardboard. Mom and Uncle MJ were visibly much more shaken. Mom said she hadn't realized just how much Aunt Trudy had meant to her.

"She was there for me when our mother wasn't. I just always took that for granted."

It was nice to see Mom and Uncle MJ talking, laughing, sitting next to each other on the loveseat being affectionate with each other. She used to talk about him all the time when I was growing up and I never understood why we didn't see him more.

"I want you to come out, come and see the vineyard, see Napa . . ." Uncle MJ said.

"Napa really is spectacular. You'll love it," Bill said.

Mom and I listened.

"So how's it going, Porgy?"

"Stop it," I laughed. "Nobody calls me that anymore."

"Well, I do. What do you want me to call you now that you're all grown up?" Uncle MJ teased.

I looked at my handsome uncle and told him that he, only he, could still call me Porgy.

"So, how are you? I heard all about your new venture. Is there anything I can do?"

"Of course."

"What? Money? Yeah, I'll make a donation."

"Thanks, that would be great."

"So I want to meet this Miles."

"Of course," I said, looking around, not seeing Miles. "I'll introduce you. So, how're things with you?"

"Great," Bill interjected, adding that they have their first white wine, a chardonnay, coming out this fall.

"You should come out for the launch. We're having a big party. Camille, you'd love Napa. It's green and peaceful."

"And very un-P.C.," Uncle MJ added. "But please come anyway."

"What's un-P.C. about it?" Mom asked.

"Well, all the brown people do the labor, grape pickers, sorters at the vibrating tables," Bill admitted.

"Who are they, Mexicans primarily?"

"Yeah, but now they're Ecuadorians, Columbians, but we pay them."

"Benefits?" Mom asked.

"We're working on it. . . . Please come, you can stay with us; maybe you can even convince Mom to come. She's never seen our place," Uncle MJ said.

"Okay," Mom said. "I'll have to work on Mom, but it could be good for her to have a trip to look forward to, you know she only traveled with Aunt Trudy."

"Hey, baby," I said, as Miles walked up where we were all sitting in a semicircle.

"Hey there," Miles said, sitting down on a folding chair next to me.

"We were just talking about going out to Napa, to my uncle's. . . . Here, meet my uncle MJ, his partner Bill."

Uncle MJ, Bill and Miles stand up to shake hands. Mom and I stand up to join the conversation.

"I've heard a lot about you," Uncle MJ says to Miles.

"Oh yeah? I hope it was true."

They all laughed, talked about wine, San Francisco, great restaurants in the Bay Area. Uncle MJ and Miles discovered they knew a few people from the finance world in common.

"I was just telling Por . . . Aisha, that you should come out in the fall when we're having a party for our new wine."

"Ah, that sounds good. So you're in Napa, not Sonoma?"

"Napa," we all say in unison.

"Ah, I love that place, love to come."

"Great," Uncle MJ and Bill say, in unison.

"So how long have you two been together?" Bill asked.

Miles put his arm around me and I him and we looked at each other, trying to approximate a length of time.

"About a year?"

"It's been almost two," I corrected.

"Man, you know women always know to the minute," Uncle MJ teased.

"So how long have you and Bill been together?" Mom asked.

"Um, fifteen years?" Uncle MJ said.

"It'll be seventeen next month," Bill said.

"So much for your theory, bro," Mom said. We all laughed. Abby walked up and joined us.

"Miles, I want you to meet *mon petite chou,* Abby."

"Ah, yes, Grandmama Abby. It's lovely to finally meet you."

"And you are Miles. You are as charming as I'd imagined."

Uncle MJ stepped to Abby and introduced himself, reminding her that he knew Adam and telling her how sorry he was to hear about his death.

"Oh, thank you, dear, but look at what he's given me." She reached out to me and kissed my forehead. "Precious Aisha and wonderful Camille."

"Yes, it's great. Well, welcome to the family," Uncle MJ said, kissing her on each cheek.

Mom had wandered off and was talking in a corner with Richard Paul.

"Those two seem to be getting along like a house on fire," Abby said of the two.

"Now you have to find one like that for me. Miles, do you know any nice bohemians my age?" Abby said.

"Miss Abby, I don't, but I'll keep you mind," Miles said.

"So, can you answer my question yet?" Abby whispered to me.

I looked at her questioning, not having a clue what she was talking about.

"Does he know your worth?"

I smiled and looked at him.

"I can say he does."

Daddy came over and pulled me off to the side.

"Who's that guy your mom's with?"

I looked at my dad and saw that he was agitated.

"You jealous, Daddy?"

He looked at me like that was a ridiculous notion and said of course not.

"I just want to know who she's spending her time with, that's all. I'm concerned about her."

"His name is Richard Paul, he's a photographer. I met him in Paris—"

"So you introduced them?"

I nod proudly and my dad looks at me.

"Why'd you do something like that?"

"'Cause I thought he was nice and that they'd like each other, which they do."

"Well, I don't know, he seems a little . . ."

"What, Daddy?"

"I don't know, something," he said and walked away.

I go after him and find Grandma sitting in the den, surrounded by members from her church and her pastor. She sat, sort of rocking back and forth in her seat as people talked and ate and drank Jack Daniels. Marjorie Blessitt sat next to her, patting her hand.

Grandma was putting on a good face, but she had a far-off look in her eyes.

I kneeled before her and she looked at me and smiled.

"How you doin', baby?"

"I'm fine, Grandma, how're you doing?"

"Oh, I'm fine, I'm fine. I probably need to eat a little something, my blood sugar feels a little low."

"Don't move. I'll fix you a plate and bring it right back."

She tried to protest, but Mrs. Blessitt held her hand a little more firmly and Grandma stayed put.

I bumped into Richard Paul on my way to the food table and told him how nice it was to see him again and thanked him for coming.

"I need to thank you."

"For?"

"For introducing me to your mom, she's a great woman."

"I told you."

"Well, yes, but you didn't tell me that your stepdad was still in love with her."

"What are you talking about?"

"Well, old Lem took me aside and instructed me that I'd better be good to Camille or. . . ."

"Oh, he's just kidding around."

"I don't think so. I could see it in his eyes. A man recognizes it in another man, believe me."

I wanted to laugh, but saw that Richard Paul was being very serious.

"Look, I've gotta fix my grandma a plate, I'll be back."

As I was putting yams, macaroni and cheese, chicken, roast beef and greens on the plate, Miles came up and whispered in my ear to meet him outside.

I delivered the plate to Grandma, with a big glass of sweet tea, and watched her take a few bites.

"Um, those yams—that Mabel knows she can make some yams."

"You okay?"

"Yes, yes, baby, thank you."

I went to the side door and found Miles sitting on one of Grandma's little benches.

"So how 'bout we get married in Napa?"

He said it like, *How 'bout we play some golf in Napa or hit some tennis balls.*

"Married? Did you say married?"

"Ish, you know I'm not a 'get on the knee, present the ring' kind of guy. You know that's where we're headin'. We've known that since the day we met. You can pick out whatever kind of ring you want. I saw something I liked, but who knows, you're the one who has to wear it and you should be happy with it—"

He was rambling now and I realized for the first time since I've known him that he was actually nervous.

"Yes, I'd love to get married, in Napa or Nebraska or wherever as long as it's to you." Miles smiled at me and we kissed. "I could care less what kind of ring I have or what kind of dress or any of that. I just want to be with you, to talk to you every day, to hear what you think, how you feel and for you to listen to me. I want to do that for the rest of my life."

"You think we could take care of each other?"

I looked at this man, this full-grown man who I could honestly say, I loved his dirty drawers and said, "Absolutely."

We looked deeply into each other's soul.

"So should we tell everybody now or what?"

"Let me check on Grandma; if she seems okay, then let's tell them."

We went back inside and found that the crowd had dispersed.

I found Grandma and Abby talking.

"You know, nobody knows what grief feels like unless they've been through it," Abby said.

"Ain't that the truth," Grandma said.

"I felt like the ground had been taken away when Adam died. Groundless, just groundless was how I felt. It's how I still feel some days."

"Yes, I don't know what I'm going to do without my Trudy. I just can't believe that I'll never hear that voice again. She'd start everything with *Now, VeVe.* I'm gonna miss her somethin' awful."

Abby stepped toward Grandma and enveloped her, saying something softly into her ear. I saw Grandma let herself be hugged, looking peaceful.

Now would be a good time.

We made the announcement surrounded by my family.

Everyone said congratulations and my dad cried in mock horror.

"Not another fifty grand!"

"No, Daddy, we're doing something very small and simple and we'll pay for it ourselves."

"Well, you ain't gotta do that, I can handle it," he said, now his feelings hurt.

"Lem, let them pay for what they want," Mom said.

"Let's have a toast. I think I saw a bottle of champagne around here," Uncle MJ said to no one in particular.

Grandma said there was always some kind of liquor in this house.

"Stuff just left over from Major. Somebody was always sending him somethin', let me go look in the pantry. You come with me, MJ."

## Camille

I watched my little girl beam as she stood next to her Miles and wished that the kind of happiness she felt at this moment she could hold in her heart always.

"I just need to borrow him, for one minute," I said, taking Miles by the arm.

Uh-oh, someone said and everyone laughed.

Miles dutifully came with me into another room.

"I hope you're not upset that I didn't come to you first," Miles said.

"No, no, I don't believe in such, although Lem will probably give you a talking to about that."

"Oh, damn, I knew I shoulda said something to him first."

"Don't worry about it, it's not like we haven't been down this road before. If it'd been the first time, you woulda had hell to pay."

"Well, that's a relief. So, what's on your mind?"

"I just have one question I've been dying to know."

"Ask away."

"Why now? Why haven't you done it before now?"

"That's an excellent question and I wish I had an answer for you. All I can say is it took me a little longer to become the person that I wanted to be."

"And who is that. I hope you don't think—"

"Camille, please," he held up his hand to say stop. "Look I understand Ish is your baby, but she's not a little girl. I guess I just finally feel at peace with myself. I don't feel the need to keep climbing that mountain, I feel like I can finally trust somebody enough to let them in and a lot of that frankly was because of Ish and how sure she was."

"Yeah, she knows how to get what she wants."

"For me it was a lot of little things, like when she insisted on going to Memphis with me to put flowers on my mother's grave, that kind of did it for me. She knew it was important without me having to say it, that it was gonna be hard, that losing my mother has been the toughest thing in my life—and she wanted to be there for me.

"I'd be lying if I didn't say that her turning her back to Will and all that wealth didn't add to her appeal."

"Yes, I have to say I was very proud of her for that. I wasn't sure she had that in her."

"She really is a remarkable young woman."

"I have to tell you that I'm a little concerned about the age difference; I mean you only a few years younger than me."

We both chuckled uncomfortably at first.

"Yeah that's a valid concern. I wouldn't want my daughter to be pushing around some old dude when she's still young, but the fact is we want to be together more than we want anything else. She keeps me interested because she keeps growing and she's not afraid. I love that about her and I think she sees something similar in me."

"Miles, I can see why she wants to be with you. You're a very impressive man, but surely there was somebody along the way that you could've hooked up with."

"Yeah, there were, but the timing wasn't right for me. I'll say it in another way, it's taken me a little while to finally grow up."

"And of course it doesn't hurt that she's beautiful—"

"Yes, but that and a token . . ." he said, tipping his head toward me, letting me know that he's had lots of beauties. "My mother used to say, beauty is as—"

"Beauty does. Your mother is so right."

We sat quiet for a moment, just taking each other in.

"I hope I've cleared things up a little. I don't want you worrying. I'm very serious about your daughter. I'm committed to her."

"Miles, I believe that."

## Geneva

"So, Mom, I want you to come out to California to see our vineyard. Camille and Porgy are going to come and Abby and Miles. What do you think?"

I was trying to remember where I'd put those bottles.

"MJ, get up on that stepladder and see if they're on that

shelf," I said, looking upward but not being able to see what I was looking for.

He got up and looked but there was nothing.

"Mom, what do you think?"

"MJ, I'm looking for something now, why you worrying me about coming all the way out there?"

"Okay, is there someplace else we should look?"

I stood there thinking of places I put things when I'm trying to put them away so I won't forget where I put them.

"Try the basement, that little room off where the pool table is."

I stood at the top of the steps waiting to give him more instructions.

"When's the last time somebody came down here?"

"Do you see it?"

"Not yet, but I'm looking for something to push through all the spiderwebs."

It was so nice to have him home again. He was always such a happy boy, so much easier than my girl. Boys are simple and girls are complex but at the end of it all I'm glad I had them both.

"Here, I got it."

Oh good, I thought, realizing I didn't have a clue as to where else to look.

He walked back up the stairs holding two dusty champagne bottles.

"We'll just wash these off and see what we have here."

I looked at my big, handsome son and grabbed his face in my hands and kissed both checks as I haven't done since he was off to kindergarten.

"I'm so glad you're here."

MJ looked at me like I'd just stripped naked in front of him.

"I'm glad I could be here too, Mom. Now, what can I use to wash these off?"

I got the glasses and put them on a tray. I handed him two dish towels.

"Hey, maybe we can do it at Uncle MJ's vineyard," I heard Aisha say from the living room.

I made my way out of the kitchen with MJ carrying the tray filled with champagne glasses.

"What's all the excitement about?"

"Looks like Aisha and Miles have an announcement to make."

"Well, Camille, we know they gonna get married."

"Yes, Grandma, and we'd like to do it at Uncle MJ and Bill's vineyard. Doesn't that sound great?"

Grandma looked at her son and her son's lover with compassion in her eyes, as if she were looking at the boy he was, her golden boy, for the first time. She looked at me. "Yes, baby, that's sounds just great."

Richard Paul and Mom were standing next to each other and I brought Miles over to them.

"Miles, I want to introduce you to Richard Paul Brown, he's the photographer I met in Paris."

"Yes, yes," Miles said, sticking out his hand to shake.

"It's a pleasure to meet you, brother. I've heard so much."

Miles looked at me with a fake aw-shucks look on his face.

"Yes, well, you know how they do, bro." They did that pump fist and laughed more heartily than seemed necessary.

Mom and I looked at each other.

"So, congratulations. I feel like this has been in the making for some time," Richard Paul said.

"Yes, yes, we're gonna jump that broom," Miles said, pulling me toward him.

"I wish you all the happiness."

"Thank you, Richard Paul, thank you very much. I think Ish and I will be very happy."

"You better be," Mom added, "or you gone have some folks to answer to that you really don't want all up in your business."

"Here, here," added Lem.

We all laughed.

"You know, I hear Camille can fight," Richard Paul said, laughing.

"I know, and Grandma has already shown me her gun," Miles said.

"So," Abby joins us, "when are we planning this grand occasion?"

"Oh, boy, the other grandma," Miles said.

"That's right, I'm the other one, so . . ."


## *Aisha*

Miles and I looked at each other. We hadn't really discussed dates or style or any of the things I was so preoccupied with before. I didn't care about a dress, a ring, a place. I just wanted Miles. I felt so calm and content. I had everything I wanted.

"We don't need anything grand?" I said to Miles.

"She's right. We have what we want," Miles said, looking at me.

"Maybe we'll just do it by the end of the summer."

"So soon?" Mom practically bellowed.

"What? You want to plan something?" I asked her sarcastically.

"Um, no. It's just that it's summer already."

"And?" Miles said.

"Well, that's so soon."

"The only hitch is, I was trying to figure out how I could get to visit Addis Ababa, Ethiopia, in the next few months, but other than that, the wedding will be a small, simple thing."

"I can't believe my ears. Is this my daughter Aisha," Camille said, pretending to check her forehead.

What was the lesson? When you have what you want you don't need all the bells and whistles.

As much as I'd like to go off on my trip, meet some of the women and Dr. Hamlin, give away some dresses, head wraps, flip-flops and earrings, come back and marry the man I loved, I knew I had to deal with Cedra.

She was there at Aunt Trudy's wake because it was the right thing to do, as a friend. You show up. You show up when you're too busy, when you're out of town, when you don't have any money—even if you can't physically be there—you are there. I appreciated her effort, but I didn't love her like I once did. My feelings had been soured by her feelings of envy and her being judgmental. Maybe I'd get past it, but right now I wasn't there. Cedra had left before Miles and I made our announcement so I'd still have to call her. Miles said to let it pass, that time would make things look better, that our friendship had been too deep to just walk away. I don't know. I had gotten used to not talking to her much, not seeing her because she worked all the time. Now it was me who was working all the time and when I wasn't working, I was happily with Miles, but now she needed me. She needed our friendship. I didn't know how to say it, that I wasn't angry at her, that I still cared, but that things had changed for me. I know that she is a part of me. She's shared my childhood, knows my secrets, my fears, my pain in ways nobody else does. That's worth saving, I suppose.

Grandma and Aunt Trudy were friends for almost sixty years. I asked Grandma if they'd ever fought, ever stopped speaking to each other.

She laughed at me and said, "Of course. One time we didn't speak for almost a year and I can honestly tell you that I can't remember why. I know she didn't think I should've broken off with the boy I was engaged to in college. She thought Major was a bad risk. A musician, no way, and jazz, that music that nobody half understands anyway. She agreed that Grandpa was a fox, now, don't misunderstand, but she didn't think he'd make a good husband. She just knew he'd be out there foolin' around, which as far as I know he didn't. I think maybe Grandpa had gotten a lotta that foolishness out of his system by the time we married. Shoot, he was thirty-one-years old. After a while, though, I know Trudy came to love Major just as everybody else did. We'd had a little party on our fifth wedding anniversary and Trudy took me aside and said she was glad that I didn't listen to her. You'd a been bored outta your cotton pickin' mind if you'd married that Kenneth. What was I thinking? We had a good laugh about that one, even though back in those days people didn't get married thinking it was supposed to be fun. It just was duty and family, but she and I both knew we needed a little more than that to get us through. Her Herbert was a pill, even though he seemed uptight. He had a straight job and everything. He was in insurance, but he loved to have a good time, was crazy about Major and he and Trudy were constantly going and doing things in all kind of organizations—his fraternity—and whatnot.

"You don't marry someone, dear heart, because you think you ought to, you marry the one you think you got to."

So maybe this was our little break. Maybe Cedra and I would be like Aunt Trudy and Grandma, not speak for a while, and then find our way back to each other.


Miles and I planned our wedding via e-mails and the phone. We didn't actually see the place until we arrived for the ceremony. One of Uncle MJ's friends, a gay Episcopalian priest, married us and we were surrounded by only our closest friends and family. All my people were there and on Miles's side, Mr. Banks came all the way from Memphis, Natasha flew up from L.A. and his close friend Brenda came in from Chicago. The wedding was outside on a patio overlooking the vast green fields with a light wind and perfect eighty degrees. I wore a cream-colored slip dress, sexy, simple, that I'd picked up in a department store. I carried pink tea roses. My mom was my maid of honor and was stunning in a fitted brown silk sheath and Daddy couldn't keep his eyes off her. They'd left their significant others at home and Miles was convinced they were going to end up back together. Daddy had insisted on a private audience with Miles and me so he could just make sure Miles understood what was expected of him.

Daddy said, "I like you, man, you remind me of me."

"Mr. McCovney—"

"Call me Lem, son, we family now."

"Lem, I take that as a great compliment. You don't have to worry, sir, I will take the finest care of Aisha."

"She's a princess, you know?"

"Daddy . . ."

"No, no, he's right. I do understand, sir. Only the best for Aisha."

"That's my boy," Daddy said, patting Miles on the back.

I wore Grandma's sapphire ring and Abby's pearls. I carried a small folded sheet of paper where I'd written the names of all the female ancestors we knew, Mama Sadie, Great-great-grandma Bert and the names of all the women I'd met in Addis Ababa whose lives I'd helped to change. I felt my life had been changed by some force that I couldn't see but I knew that these women whose names I held in my hand had something to do with how things had turned out for me.

I wanted them all, the ones who came before and the ones yet to be, to know the kind of fullness I felt right now, what was possible for their lives too. For all this good fortune wasn't just happening to me. It was about all of us.

Mabel, the lady who helps Grandma clean, got herself out all the way to Napa Valley, California too. She'd never been on an airplane before. Grandma wanted her to be there, because she knew I meant something to Mabel, who had watched me grow up.

She sat in the sun and beamed when the service was over.

Mmm, I-esh-a sure did do it right. Got herself a good job and married somebody she really loved, ain't she somethin'?

How 'bout that.

# ABOUT THE AUTHOR

BENILDE LITTLE is the bestselling author of the novels *Good Hair* (selected as one of the ten best books of 1996 by the *Los Angeles Times*), *The Itch,* and *Acting Out.* A former reporter for *People* and senior editor at *Essence,* she lives in Montclair, New Jersey, with her husband and two children.